I0775057

Bride of Wolffang
Book 1 of the Wolffang Saga
JS Williams

JS Williams, LLC

Copyright © 2025 by JS Williams

All rights reserved.

Printed in The United States.

ISBN: 978-1-970280-04-3

Published by: JS Williams, LLC

No part of this publication may be reproduced, distributed, or transmitted in any form or by any means, including photocopying, recording, or other electronic or mechanical methods, or by any information storage and retrieval system without the prior written permission of the publisher, except in the case of very brief quotations embodied in critical reviews and certain other noncommercial uses permitted by copyright law.

This is a work of fiction. Names, characters, business, events and incidents are the products of the author's imagination. Any resemblance to actual persons, living or dead, or actual events is purely coincidental.

Editor: Sara Bierling

Cover design: JS Williams

Contents

Dedication

To my husband, Greg, who encouraged me to pursue publishing my first book.

Acknowledgement

I want to acknowledge my best friends, Sara H, Jennie, Leah, and Michelle, who read my first drafts for me, as well as my editor/friend Sara B who gave me encouragement and insight throughout the entire writing process.

Chapter 1

HARPER Deveraugh stepped off the plane in San Francisco. It had been a couple of years since she had seen her half-brother, Michael. This was her first time visiting him here in San Francisco as he had always visited her in Boston. She had been busy with college on the East Coast, and he with his business. He owned a property investment compa-ny and had done well for himself. They had kept in touch by text, phone, and video calls. Michael had called her last week asking her to come visit him, saying he had some important news that he had to tell her in person. Michael was older than her by five years but raised by her mother after their parents had married when he was 2 years old. Almost two years ago, they lost their parents in a car accident. He was all the family she had now.

Harper adjusted her worn college backpack over her shoulder and collected her suitcase from the carousel, then headed to the airport exit. Michael had told her he would have someone there to pick her up. At the exit of the airport, she looked for a name card and walked over to the man holding it. He was quite handsome, stood a head taller than her, with a neatly trimmed short beard/mustache combination, short dark brown wavy hair, brown eyes, olive-toned skin, and had dressed in a casual, fitted suit.

Laken Howlkind looked up from his watch to see a woman walking towards him. She had blond hair cut in a layered bob, blue eyes, fair skin, and was petite. The top of her head came just to his shoulder. She wore a pair of blousy pants with a thin belt and a tank top tucked into the pants covered with a criss-cross style, cropped sweater.

When she got closer to Laken, he picked up a scent that made his wolf, Enzo, howl. It was a combination of vanilla and lavender. *That is our mate. You must claim her. She belongs to us.*

A human is my mate? He thought. While not unheard of, it was rare, especially for an Alpha. Enzo repeated, *She's ours. Take and mark her now!*

Calm now, Laken told Enzo. *You know you're being unreasonable. We're in an open public place and don't even know who she is.* Though he could feel the pull to her, the need to touch her, the desire to kiss her, and the want to have her in his life. Someone explained the mate bond's pull to him this way. However, he hadn't expected the feeling to be so strong.

Harper stepped up to the man and said, "I'm Harper Deveraugh. I believe you're here to drive me to my brother's?"

Laken, startled, thought, *My mate is Michael's sister?* She looked very much like his friend Michael, despite them being only half siblings. He responded, "Yes, I'm a friend of your brother. My name is Laken Howlkind." He reached out his hand.

Harper took Laken's hand. She gasped and looked him in the eyes as she felt a spark between the two of them. She tried to pull her hand away.

Laken grasped her hand harder. *How did she feel it too?* Laken wondered. He could see the were-wolf-mate bond weave around their wrists and up their arms, but he knew she couldn't. He knew she couldn't see it, but she could feel that something was happening between them.

Harper pulled her hand away from his, tucked a piece of hair behind her ear, and crossed her arms in front of her. Laken folded the sign with her name on it and placed it in his pocket, along with his hand.

"Follow me," he said. "Your brother is waiting for us at his house." Laken led her out to his car.

The car ride to Michael's place was quiet. Laken and Harper were both engrossed in their thoughts.

Laken was the Alpha of the San Francisco Area werewolf pack. His pack differed from most others, and many North American tribes scorned it. While most lived on large tracts of land in remote areas, his lived among humans in one of the largest cities in the US. Many didn't agree that living among humans was a good idea.

Laken started the San Francisco Area pack twelve years ago when he was 16 years old, beginning with mostly rogue wolves who lacked their own. He had lost his pack when his parents died, and he had become a rogue himself. Settling in San Francisco when he was younger had been a strategic decision, because it made werewolves easier to hide. As his pack had grown, he had found that it was one of the best decisions he had made.

Now his was one of the largest packs in North America. Most of the werewolves from the pack worked at Wolffang Enterprises, the company that Laken had started and was CEO of. Wolffang Enterprises also employed many humans as well. Some called the San Francisco Area pack the Wolffang pack because of the connection between it and his business.

Because his pack lived in the human world, he didn't think that his mate being human would be an issue. How to explain to Harper that she was his mate, and he a werewolf, would be the bigger issue. The werewolf world remained hidden from humans, and werewolves rarely allowed humans into their inner circle.

There was so much stigma and negativity surrounding werewolves because of history and modern publications. Most literature wasn't accurate about the species. Each werewolf had a wolf spirit that lived within him or her, but it didn't wake until after they turned 16 years old. Once connected with the wolf spirit, a werewolf could shift into a wolf at will. Initially, werewolves shifted because it was new and fun, but as they aged, they shifted more out of necessity for battles or runs.

Werewolves were stronger than humans in all ways - physically, emotionally, mentally, and even romantically. Werewolves rarely married except to their mates. Many werewolves would wait years until they found their mate, indulging in short-term relationships to ease the burden of loneliness. Lycans believed that the Moon Goddess sent one person to be their lifelong companion, a mate that would fit each person and his/her wolf. A werewolf would smell and connect with his or her mate, as he had done with Harper. However, usually it was another werewolf, and they recognized the connection together. Once they had found each other, they would be instantly as well as madly attracted to each other. Usually, love would quickly follow, though not always. If a pair of mated werewolves didn't fall in love and wanted to break their bond, they could reject each other, but this would cause intense pain.

Harper had never believed in love at first sight. She still didn't. Lust at first touch — now that was something she might believe in. But she never considered herself to be something like that. She was just too level-headed. Maybe it was because she had never really been in love. She always focused too much on her studies. How else could she explain that feeling, though, when she and Laken touched hands?

She had felt an immediate physical pull, but it was more than that. It felt like she had wanted to be with him for the rest of her life. Why would that be? Harper had only just met Laken. She shouldn't feel such an immediate connection to him. Instead, she wanted to find out all she could about him, touch him, kiss him. She glanced over at him and bit her lip. Wait, what was she thinking?

The car pulled into Michael's driveway, and this snapped both Harper and Laken out of their thoughts. As the car stopped, Michael opened the front door and stepped out of the house. Laken got out of the car first and opened the door for Harper.

Michael was standing at the door, and Harper immediately ran up and hugged him. He hugged her back, laughing.

"It's so good to see you! Thank you so much for coming," he exclaimed.

Harper said, "Let me go get my luggage." She turned back to the car, just in time to see Laken set her luggage down next to her.

"Oh, thank you. I was just coming to get that," she told Laken.

Laken smiled and stated, "You're welcome. It was no trouble."

Harper looked away as his smile made her feel warm inside. She went to take the handle of her suitcase, and her hand brushed his. Again, that spark went from his skin to hers. She pulled her hand back quickly and glanced his way to see him looking at her. Did he feel it too?

"Let's go inside. Dinner will be ready for us soon. Did you want to freshen up, Harper?" Michael looked at Harper with the question. "I'll share some news with both of you after dinner."

Harper said quickly, "Yes, I'd like to clean up, and then I'll be down. Can you show me to my room?"

Michael replied, "Laken, can you take her luggage to the guest room for me? You know where it is."

Laken looked at Michael questioningly, but said, "Of course. Harper?" He beckoned her to follow him. He wondered what Michael was up to, asking him to show Harper to the guest room as if he were the chauffeur or something.

Laken picked up Harper's luggage, then led Harper into the house and up the stairs. He stopped at the door of a bedroom. Setting the suitcase inside the doorway, he gave a slight bow with a half smile.

Harper said, "Thank you. I'll see you at dinner soon." She entered the room and shut the door. Inside, she leaned on it and took a deep breath. Why did he affect her like this? She had been in a few relationships, two fairly serious. None had reached the point of becoming intimate, though. One smile, even a simple touch, from Laken and all thoughts flew out the window. What would happen if he actually kissed her? She wondered.

Laken joined Michael downstairs in the dining room. He immediately went over to the bar and poured himself a whiskey on the rocks. Michael looked at him and asked, "Are you okay?"

"Fine. Why do you ask?" asked Laken in return.

Michael eyed the glass in Laken's hand as a reply and lifted an eyebrow. "Well, you rarely drink before dinner."

"Did you see me drink any yet? All I did was pour it," Laken said as he swirled the liquor in the glass.

He had to get a grip on himself. Even Michael was noticing his control slipping.

Laughter from Michael followed him as he sat at the table.

Harper entered, asking, "What's so funny?"

Laken scowled as Michael continued laughing. "Nothing. Come and sit. Let's eat. Would you like a drink?"

"I'll have a glass of white wine, if you have some," Harper replied.

"Of course," Michael told Harper. "Laken, can you go get the bottle from the wine fridge and pour her a glass? I'll serve dinner now."

Laken got up and poured a glass of wine for Harper. He set it down on the table in front of her, then took his seat across the table from her. Michael took his seat at the head of the table.

Dinner proceeded with the conversation revolving around Harper and Michael catching up. Laken listened while they talked about their lives. He knew the two of them were close, but he enjoyed hearing more about the woman who was his mate.

They laughed over the story of Michael and Harper getting grounded for pranking their mother.

Michael had been the one to come up with the idea, but both of them had been involved. They had taken their mom's clothes when she was in the shower and left her with just a towel, but also locked the bedroom door so she couldn't get her clothes. Their mom hadn't thought it as funny as they had, so they had gotten grounded for two days.

Harper shared how some of her parents' neighbors in Boston were doing. She kept in touch with them even after moving and had dinner once a month at their home. She told Michael that Mr. and Mrs. Locklyn were both doing well, though, of course, getting older. Harper would have dinner with them again the following week when she returned to Boston. Michael asked her to give them his regards.

Michael asked Harper about her schooling and thesis. She explained she was starting the background research for her thesis and had three classes for the semester. One of her classes was a continuation of her minor in French. She explained to Laken that knowing French was helpful for her reading many of the manuscripts that she needed for her thesis.

Laken envied Michael and Harper's sibling bond. As an only child, he had never had such. His mate also amazed him, as he learned she was a woman who cared for others and shared a special connection with her brother and friends.

As dinner ended, Michael asked Laken and Harper to join him in the living room. The three moved to the other room and took seats around the coffee table. Harper sat with Michael on the couch, and Laken sat in an accent chair.

"I brought both of you here to talk to you about something," Michael began. "You two are the most important people in my life. Laken, Harper is the only family that I've left. And Harper, Laken is my closest friend."

Michael paused, "I won't sugarcoat this, as there is no easy way to say it. Two months ago, doctors diagnosed me with inoperable stage 4 brain cancer. They have given me six months to live, at most."

Harper gasped and put her hand to her mouth, and Michael put his arm on her shoulder. Laken went to stand up, but Michael put his hand out, indicating that he should sit back down.

Michael explained, "Fortunately, I'm not experiencing any effects right now, but the doctor said the cancer is aggressive, spreading fast, and my condition will deteriorate quickly."

"I don't understand. You look and seem fine. What is the basis for your prognosis?" Harper asked, her lips quivering.

"Glioblastoma is characterized by its quick growth and its ability to destroy healthy cells," Michael elaborated.

By this time, tears were streaming down Harper's face. "Please, Harper, I've accepted my diagnosis. Now, I need to put my affairs in order. That's why the two of you are here."

Looking at his best friend, Michael continued, "Laken, I can't leave Harper in the world alone. I want you to marry and take care of her for me. You're the only person I can trust my sister with. I'm leaving all my money to her since I know you don't need it. I would also like you to buy out my business, as I trust you to run it as I would and take care of the employees."

Harper's mouth fell open in disbelief. "Michael, you can't expect me to marry a total stranger!"

Laken interrupted, "Yes, Michael, I will. To both."

Both Michael and Harper turned to look at Laken incredulously.

Harper exclaimed, "What? Why would you do this?"

"I don't have a wife, and Michael is my best friend. This is the least I can do for him." Laken replied.

"Great!" Michael said. "It's all set, and a relief for me to know that you'll be there for Harper. Why don't we all meet tomorrow to complete everything?"

"What about what I want?" exclaimed Harper. "You just expect me to give up my life in Boston and marry your best friend? I understand you want to take care of me, but I'm an adult."

"Please do it for me, Harper," pleaded Michael. "I need to know that I've taken care of you and kept you safe before I die."

Harper questioned, "What about school and my research? I'm only 2 weeks into the semester; it just started. You can't expect me to drop everything and move to San Francisco."

"You can switch to a university here to continue your thesis and schooling," Laken cut in.

Pointing at him, Harper's tone became harsh, "I don't need your input. I don't even know you. Today was the first day I met you. You can't expect me to marry you based on knowing you for, what, four hours?"

"I can support you financially and am considered to be quite the catch. Your brother can vouch for both," Laken interrupted her tirade. "I would hope that you realize I'm not doing this on a whim, either. I'm doing it for Michael and you."

Harper looked from Laken to Michael. It was two to one. She wouldn't get support from either of them. Still reeling from the news of Michael's diagnosis, she was unprepared to fight over this. She would agree to it for now and figure out a way out of it later.

Harper hung her head and said, "Fine, I'll do it. For you, Michael."

Chapter 2

MICHAEL watched his sister as she left the living room to head upstairs. She had pleaded fatigue after the flight and his revelation. He knew she was upset with his pressuring her to marry his best friend. Reaching up, he scrubbed his hand across his face.

He sighed and looked at Laken. "Thank you for agreeing to my request. I thought that I would have had to do more convincing for you to go along with it."

Laken looked at the man who had been his friend since college. He couldn't tell Michael that Harper was his mate and destined to be with him; he'd agreed for that reason, not because Michael had asked. Michael didn't know Laken was a werewolf, and he wouldn't understand the mate bond.

"Our friendship has lasted for eight years, and we're like brothers. If I can do this for you to protect your sister, I will," Laken explained in a way that he hoped would appease his friend.

Michael and Laken spent the next quarter of an hour in small talk before Laken left for the night. Walking him to the door, Michael said goodbye, then closed the door and watched his friend walk to his car through the side window.

Knowing he would have to deal with Harper in the morning, Michael trudged up the stairs to his bedroom. He had to make her understand he was doing this for her own good. With both their parents gone, and his own departure imminent, he needed to ensure her well-being. If she had already been in a relationship with a good man, he wouldn't have had to resort to this. He hoped that Harper and Laken would eventually find love together, or at least be a good match.

The next day, Laken was in his office at Wolffang Enterprises earlier than usual. He had already made a list of things he needed to do and even checked off a couple before Tatum walked in. Tatum was the Beta or second in command of the wolf pack. He was also his executive assistant at Wolffang Enterprises, as well as his closest friend next to Michael. Laken had met Tatum as another rogue living on the streets of San Francisco when he was 17 years old. The two had connected and started the pack together, with Laken as alpha and Tatum as beta.

Michael didn't know Laken was a werewolf. Humans were not let into the werewolf world. It had hurt him not to share that part of himself with Michael, but it was safer for Michael. Had he not discovered that Harper had been his mate, then he would have had to deny his friend the request to marry her.

Tatum cleared his throat and snapped his fingers in front of Laken's face. Laken looked at him. Tatum smiled and said, "Alpha, I don't know what you were thinking about, but I've asked you twice what brought you in to work early today."

Looking sheepish, Laken replied, "I'm meeting with Michael and his sister at 10am, so I needed to get some things done early. Congratulate me, I'm getting married."

"What?!" exclaimed Tatum. "To whom?"

"Michael's sister, Harper," said Laken, looking Tatum in the eyes. "She's my mate, and Michael has terminal cancer. He has asked me to take care of her and wants us married before he gets worse."

Tatum sank into the chair on the other side of Laken's desk. "Alpha, wait. You've found your mate. And she's Michael's sister, a human. Plus Michael is dying?" He shook his head. "This is too much."

"I know. Michael also asked me to buy out his company and take it over. He wants to meet to go over more details. I'll need to meet with the werewolf council to let them know that I've found my mate and will get married. Soon. I don't think there'll be an issue with Harper being a human, but I need to follow proper protocol," Laken explained.

Tatum replied, "Of course, Alpha. What do you need me to do?"

Laken answered, "Can you please set up the meeting with the werewolf council for the next few days? I also need you to contact City Hall and find out when there are open times over the next week and a half for Harper and me to get married. Right now, it looks like I'm going to buy an engagement ring."

Laken and Harper met Michael at his business in a conference room. Michael had asked his lawyer to join them as well. The lawyer sat next to Michael on one side of the table, with Laken and Harper on the other side. Harper glanced at Laken and shifted her chair so she wasn't too close to him. She dared not risk touching him as being so near to him was distracting enough. Laken noticed and gave her a sideways look. Michael cleared his throat to gain their attention. "Let's start by signing the documents selling and transferring the MD Group to Laken. After that, my lawyer can leave."

"Sounds good to me," replied Laken, taking the pen and signing the proffered documents in triplicate. Harper noticed he didn't even read any of the papers.

The lawyer notarized the three sets of documents and put each set in its own folder. One set went to Michael, another to Laken, and the last he kept. Standing up, he nodded to each man, and then Harper, before saying goodbye and taking his leave.

"With that settled, let's talk about your wedding plans," said Michael.

Laken interrupted, "Before we get too far into that, I want to ask Harper something."

Turning to Harper, he pushed back his chair and dropped to one knee in front of her. "I know this is not a conventional marriage, but I didn't want you to miss out on a proposal. Harper Deveraugh, would you marry me?" Laken asked as he pulled a ring box from his suit jacket pocket and opened it.

Harper's eyes went wide seeing the platinum 3 karat round diamond engagement ring in front of her. It had a baguette-cut sapphire and small diamond accents on each side of the enormous diamond. It was beautiful.

"Do you like it? If you don't, I can buy you a different ring instead." asked Laken.

Harper looked him in the eye. "I love it. And yes. Thank you for asking. Both if I wanted to marry you and if I liked the ring."

Laken's smile lit up his eyes, and he stood up, placing the ring on her finger. Her heart skipped a beat, realizing she had made him happy. *Maybe this marriage wouldn't be so bad after all. Laken is a handsome man, and there is this attraction between us or whatever you want to call it.*

They both startled, having forgotten about Michael, when he said, "Why don't you kiss her then? Since you want this to be like a proper proposal." They both looked at Michael, seeing a twinkle in his eyes, hinting at his chiding.

Laken gave in to the feelings that he had pushed aside through Michael's request. He leaned toward Harper and let his lips meet hers in a whisper-soft kiss. A zing passed between them, and Harper leaned back quickly. Michael chuckled and said jokingly, "Save it for the wedding night, you two."

Harper looked away from Laken quickly, hearing Michael's words. Every time they touched, she wondered what more would be like. Here she was thinking about his touch, yet she questioned getting married to him. The one wasn't exclusive to the other, though, because she was being forced into the marriage and her feelings were almost beyond her control.

Michael pulled her from her thoughts by asking them to move to the next agenda item. They spent the next hour planning the wedding itself. Michael would take care of the exact details. The wedding would take place in a week and a half. Laken had received a text from his executive assistant with the open dates and times for City Hall.

Harper looked at the ring on her hand. Tomorrow she flew back to Boston to settle her affairs there, pack up her belongings, and move her life to San Francisco. She felt like her life and decisions were being taken out of her control.

Back at Michael's home, Harper decided she needed to have a talk with Michael before she left. She was still uncomfortable with the thought of marrying Laken. The weight of the new engagement ring on her finger emphasized this.

Entering Michael's office, Harper found him on his laptop, doing some work. He glanced up when she entered and closed the computer after seeing the serious look on her face. Waving his arm to the wingback chairs on the other side of the desk, the two sat facing each other.

"What is it, Harper? Is something wrong?" he asked his sister.

Harper took a deep breath before demanding, "Why are you making me marry Laken? You have taken my choice away from me, and when I said no, you railroaded me."

"You're my only family, Harper. As your older brother, I must ensure your care after I'm gone. Obviously, I wouldn't have done it this way or this soon. Laken is my best friend and well-off. He's the only person I can trust with you." Michael explained.

"But why did you feel I had to marry him? Why couldn't you have just had him check in on me or be a co-owner of my money?" she countered.

Michael sighed, briefly closing his eyes before opening them again to look at Harper. "Our parents are gone, and we have no other relatives. You have no boyfriend or even the prospect of such. I've this fear that if you don't do this, then something will happen to you. It keeps me up at night. While I can't understand your feelings completely, I beg you to please do this as planned."

Harper hadn't realized the place that Michael had been coming from with his request. Now that she heard the anguish in his voice as he begged her to continue with the wedding, she knew she had to relent. She would give the marriage a chance or, if nothing else, once Michael was gone, she would divorce Laken and continue on with her life.

"Hearing you say it like that, Michael, I'll do as you ask. I hear of your love for me and understand your need to make sure I'm in a stable place." said Harper.

Michael leaned forward, embracing Harper tightly. Hugging her brother back, Harper blinked back tears. She had a wedding to prepare for and needed to decipher what she felt for Laken.

Laken looked around at the members of the werewolf council of the San Francisco Area pack. The council always met in the large boardroom at Wolffang Enterprises. It was one of the few spaces that would fit that number of people, plus it was secure and private. A male and female werewolf from each level—Elder, Beta, Gamma, and Omega—made up the council. The San Francisco Area pack was different because it allowed omegas to be on its council and to be treated as equals to other werewolves.

Typically, the Elders are the previous Alpha and Luna, but since the pack lacked a previous Alpha and Luna, the pack had asked Wells and Jora, the wisest werewolf pair, to fill this role. Their pack exiled them for defending Omegas, forcing them to become rogues. Both had what was called a "hippy" look by humans. Wells had shoulder-length white hair tied back at his nape, with gray eyes and wore loose cotton clothes. Jora was his sister, not his mate, and was much like her brother. She had long silver hair, which she often wore in a bun, with light blue eyes. Jora often wore flowing dresses that were embroidered with moons, stars, and other designs. Tatum and his mate, Elsie, made up the Betas. He was a very tall, black man with closely cut hair and brown eyes, while his mate was a thin Asian woman who was petite with shoulder-length cut straight black hair and amber eyes. Tatum wore a blue suit to the council meeting, and Elsie a green sundress. They both would go to work at Wolffang Enterprises after the meeting. The Gammas were Raegan and her mate, Colt, and the Omegas were Alana and Paxton. Raegan was a tall Hispanic woman with thick, dark brown hair pulled back into a ponytail and brown eyes. She wore leggings and a workout top as she was a personal trainer and owned her own business with her mate, Colt. He also wore workout clothes. Colt was a blond-haired, blue-eyed man who many would mistake for a surfer. Alana and Paxton were fraternal twins who also worked for Wolffang Enterprises, but at the shipping ware-house. Alana had short, curly red hair and green eyes, while her twin had wavy chestnut hair and hazel eyes. Both wore jeans and Wolffang polo shirts. Laken, as the Alpha, made up the council as well. Each person brought his or her own experiences and background, coming from different packs and having been a rogue or outcast. Once Harper became his Luna, she would also be on the council.

"I have called this council meeting to inform all of you I've found my mate. Her name is Harper Deveraugh. Before you ask, yes, she's human. She is the sister of my best friend, Michael Deveraugh. She'll be my wife, but I'm following protocol to inform the council and receive its approval," explained Laken.

Omega Paxton stood. "My Alpha, I'm sure I share most of the council's concern, not that your mate is a human, but how will you tell her about the pack and her responsibilities?"

The other council members nodded at this. Laken had expected this.

"I wish I had a complete answer for you. Unfortunately, I need to marry Harper before she and I thoroughly know each other. I hope that after we trust each other fully, I can share with her the truth of who I am, and the Moon Goddess will guide us. Michael has terminal cancer and has asked that I marry her before he passes. I wouldn't have agreed to it had I not realized that she was my mate. The mate bond has already formed. Even Harper has felt it, though she, of course, doesn't understand what she has felt."

"Considering the situation, the Moon Goddess is the only one who can see the plan. The council approves your marriage," stated Wells.

Chapter 3

TEN days later, Laken and Harper were married at City Hall in a civil ceremony with Michael as a witness, as well as Tatum, who Laken introduced to Harper as his other best friend. Before the wedding, Harper had returned to Boston and packed up all her stuff to be moved to San Francisco. She had only returned the day before.

Harper thought back to a talk she had had with her friend Megan while packing in Boston.

Open boxes and partially packed belongings filled Harper's cozy apartment. She had sat cross-legged on the floor, staring at the engagement ring on her finger. Megan had lounged on the couch, sipping coffee.

"So, let me get this straight. Your brother's dying wish is for you to marry his best friend... and you said yes?" asked Megan.

Defensively, Harper had replied, "What was I supposed to do, Megan? Say no? Michael's all I have left. He explained he wants to see me settled and safe. I tried to, but after he begged and I saw how important this was to him, I couldn't do it."

Megan had snickered in response, "I mean, Laken's hot from the photo you showed me. I'll give you that. But marriage? This is wild."

Harper looked at her friend, then down at the ring again before she spoke. "This stays between us. There's something about Laken... I can't explain it. When I look at him, I just want to get to know him better. And when he touched my hand..." sighing, Harper told her friend truthfully.

Megan grinned. "Sparks? Fireworks? A little tingle down your spine?"

Harper had picked up a pillow and threw it at her friend, "Yes, maybe. Ugh, I don't know. I feel like my life's been flipped upside down. All I know is I'm going to miss you and Boston. I don't know if I'm doing the right thing."

Michael had arranged everything for the wedding and the dinner afterward. He had bought a dress for Harper to wear, the flowers, and even arranged for the photographer. Dinner afterward was in a private room at a five-star hotel nearby. He wanted only the best for his sister's wedding.

Harper looked in the guest room mirror at Michael's house. She couldn't believe she was getting married, especially to someone she had met just over a week ago. True, there was that handshake and how it made her feel. The mirror reflected her uncertainty, but also a beautiful young woman that she didn't quite recognize. Reaching up, Harper touched a hand to her face to prove to herself that it really was her. Feeling her touch was proof that it was herself in the wedding dress getting married to an almost stranger as a promise to her dying brother. Seeing the engagement ring displayed on her hand in the mirror, part of her was excited to see what was to come between Laken and herself.

The knock on the door startled her. "Are you ready yet?" asked Michael.

"Yes, come on in," Harper replied.

The door opened, and Michael entered. His face lit up when he saw her in the wedding dress he had chosen. It was simple yet elegant, perfect for a civil wedding, but also still bridal enough to make a woman feel beautiful on her wedding day. It was ivory-colored satin with slim three-quarter-length sleeves and a deep V-neck with a mid-calf length A-line skirt that had a single petticoat underneath.

"You look beautiful," Michael said. "But there is something missing." He reached into his pocket and brought out a box. When he opened it, Harper saw a necklace with a large teardrop pearl at the center hanging on a delicate yellow gold chain. She reached out a hand, touching it. "It's gorgeous."

Michael said, "Turn around. I'll put it on you."

Harper turned back to the mirror and watched as Michael put the necklace around her neck. "Thank you so much."

"Don't thank me," said Michael. "It's a wedding gift from Laken. Ready to go?"

Her eyes widened upon hearing that Laken had bought her a wedding gift. She reached up to touch the necklace briefly. *Did he care about her?* Looking one last time in the mirror, Harper took a deep breath before taking Michael's hand and walking out of the room.

Laken waited in the City Hall office with his Beta, Tatum. Tatum had been one of the first wolves to join the pack when he had created it. He still had not figured out when and how he would tell Harper about his being a werewolf and the mate bond. He has done some research but not found much on how to do such an introduction. There wasn't a manual on the topic with the rarity of a human entering the werewolf world, especially as an alpha's mate.

He looked up as Michael entered the City Hall office with Harper. She was beautiful. His heart stopped in his chest, and his wolf whispered in his ear, "Ours." He noticed his wedding gift around her neck, and he immediately pictured his mark under it. Shaking his head slightly, he whispered to himself, "Get it together."

The ceremony seemed to be over in a blur. Soon it was time to exchange rings and seal the vows with the traditional kiss. Laken took Harper's hand, watching the mate bond weave around their hands, and slid a wedding band that matched the engage-ment ring on her finger. It had alternating round diamonds and baguette-cut sapphires in an eternity style. He heard the catch in her breathing when he took her hand and when she saw the wedding band. Laken grinned, knowing that it was his touch that caused her to feel such. His breathing sped up when she took his hand and slid a band on his finger that her brother handed to her. Matthew had bought a wedding band that matched her ring for Laken. His ring had two rows of round diamonds surrounding a middle row of baguette sapphires, and one channel set in the front.

"You may kiss the bride," said the officiant.

Laken reached for Harper's face, and his lips touched hers. The heat flared between the two of them. He wrapped his arms around her and pulled her close, deepening the kiss, inhaling her scent, which was intoxicating to him.

"Ahem," said a voice, and a hand tapped on his shoulder.

Laken practically growled until Tatum said, "Umm...Laken?"

This brought Laken back to where he was, and he pulled back from Harper. They were both out of breath. She looked at him in shock and lifted a hand to her lips.

Michael smiled at them both. "That was quite a kiss. Let's go celebrate with dinner."

Harper looked at the matched set of rings on her hand and at the man sitting next to her. What happened during the ceremony? First when they touched hands again and then that kiss? It wasn't her first kiss with Laken, but the last had been quite chaste. This one, however... She hadn't been able to stop herself from kissing him back. Nor was she the one who had stopped the kiss. Her cheeks reddened, remembering that others had had to interrupt the two of them.

She picked at her food throughout the entire dinner and made small talk. She reached out for her water glass, and when she did, her hand brushed against Laken's as he went for a roll. That sizzle of energy went up her arm again. She looked at him, and he was watching her with fire in his eyes. Harper glanced away quickly. Why couldn't she control her emotions and this feeling she had when she touched him?

"Who's ready for the wedding cake?" Michael asked.

Harper looked up. "Cake?"

"Of course! It's a tradition I couldn't let you miss," he replied, waving for the server to bring it in.

The server brought in a small cake with a heart topper and placed it in front of Harper and Laken, along with a knife. Apparently, they were expected to cut the cake together. Laken picked up the knife and held it out to Harper to help him. She placed her hand over his, again feeling that jolt. She hurried to cut the cake into pieces, then let the server take over serving the cake.

Laken placed the knife down and looked over at Harper. He couldn't get the kiss out of his head, but she could barely stand to touch him, it seemed. Every time they touched, she pulled away as quickly as possible. Was it because she couldn't stand his touch, or was it she was denying their attraction?

She was so quiet, too. He barely knew her except for what Michael had told him and what he had found out during dinner at Michael's house. He knew she was a caring person who had married him to fulfill her dying brother's wish. Her studies, her friends, and her family in Boston were her life until now, and this change had taken it all away from her. Laken wanted to know more about her–craved it, in fact–but he wasn't sure how to do it without sounding like he was being too inquisitive. And if he didn't ask, he could appear cold. He needed to find the perfect balance. If he didn't, how would it affect their relationship?

Tonight was their wedding night. He wanted to complete their mating bond and mark her, but was afraid that it would be too much for her. He would need to take this slowly; otherwise, she would never trust him.

Michael stood for one last toast. "As a gift to the married couple, I've reserved the honeymoon suite for you in this hotel. I've already packed an overnight bag for each of you and had it brought to the room. Enjoy!"

The two looked at Michael in surprise, Harper aghast. How could he do this to her? This wasn't a typical marriage. She never expected to sleep with her new husband on their wedding night.

Laken and Harper entered the honeymoon suite together after saying goodnight to Michael and Tatum. Closing the door behind them, Laken turned to Harper. "Why don't you take the bathroom first?"

Without looking at Laken, Harper said, "Thank you." She picked up her overnight bag and headed into the bathroom, but then stopped. "Oh Laken. I forgot to tell you thank you for the necklace. Could you help me take it off first?"

"Of course, and you're welcome," replied Laken. He unclasped the necklace, forcing himself to ignore her scent. He handed her the necklace and watched her disappear into the bathroom.

Laken picked up his own overnight bag and went into the bedroom. He unpacked his things and then headed to the sitting area to wait for Harper to finish in the bathroom.

In the bathroom, Harper tried to take as much time as possible before coming out. She couldn't believe that Michael had packed a sheer negligee for her. What was he up to? The bathroom mirror showed her that the lilac babydoll was see-through from the bodice down to where it brushed the backs of her thighs. Its body-hugging cups were only two layers thick, made of the overlapping sheer fabric. It had barely-there straps holding it all up and a G-string bottom that covered just the necessary parts. Harper could only imagine that Michael had ordered it online and not bought it in a store. She blushed at her own reflection. If this were her true wedding night, it would have been exactly what she would have wanted to wear. But now, she wasn't sure how she could sleep comfortably next to Laken with so little clothing on.

Laken knocked on the door. "Harper, is everything okay?"

"Yes, I'm fine. I'll be right out. Can you please turn away?" Harper asked. "My brother sent a sheer nightgown and no robe. He must be trying to force us into a situation."

"You're my wife..." Laken replied.

Harper interrupted to plead, "Please..."

Chapter 4

H ARPER stepped out of the bathroom after Laken assured her he was in the sitting room. She hurried to the bed and scrambled under the covers. "I'm in bed now," she called to Laken.

Laken immediately had a picture of her waiting for him in a skimpy bit of lace and shook his head to clear the image. He entered the bedroom, picked up the items he'd left out, and immediately went into the bathroom. It took everything he had not to look at Harper in the bed. He took a cold shower and had a talk with his wolf, Enzo, about how completing the mating bond would have to wait. It was becoming clear to him that connecting with his mate emotionally was more important.

Clad in only pajama bottoms, Laken entered the bedroom. His bare chest showed off his defined muscles. He was broad and sculpted, with dark brown chest hair that tapered down his waist over a six-pack. His well-built arms tapered from powerful upper arms to sinewy forearms.

Werewolves were naturally stronger than humans, but some, including Alphas, Betas, and Gammas, were even stronger. Alphas were the strongest mentally, physically, cognitively, and elevated in terms of status. That is why they were the pack leaders. When more than one Alpha was in a pack, they typically fought to establish dominance.

Laken turned off the light and joined Harper in the bed, sliding under the covers as well. He didn't touch Harper, despite how much he craved to do so. He turned on his side and looked towards where she lay. "Harper, I know that you only married me because your brother asked you to. I'd like us to get to know each other. I want you to know that I'm very attracted to you, but I don't want to pressure you into anything," he said to her.

He felt the bed move as Harper turned toward him. She questioned, "You are? I feel something; I'll call it attraction, though I don't understand what it is between us. I'd also like to get to know you. This is a lot of changes all at once. I'm feeling very lost and confused right now." She reached out to touch him but pulled her hand back at the very last second.

Laken grabbed her hand and held it to his chest, right over his heart. "Harper, please don't be afraid of what is between us," he pleaded.

How had he seen her try to touch him in the dark? Harper wondered and gave in to her feelings as she leaned her head on his chest and sighed. "I just don't understand it. I need time."

She felt a kiss on the top of her head. "And you have it. Now go to sleep."

The next morning, Laken woke up with Harper's head still on his chest and one of her legs resting over his. Enzo howled for him to take her. He gritted his teeth and pulled himself away from her. She moaned softly as she resettled herself. He had promised her time, and he would keep that promise.

Before taking another cold shower, he placed a room service order for breakfast. He figured by the time he finished, it would be there.

Harper awoke to the sound of the bathroom door closing. She heard the shower start and remembered that she was now married. Laken had kept his word, and nothing had happened last night. She got up and went to the closet to see if there was a robe in it. Finding one, she put it on and went into the sitting room to check out the suite, as she hadn't done so last night.

She pulled back the curtains, looking out onto San Francisco Bay. Being on the top floor, the hotel room had a beautiful view. Harper could see a park with lots of stairs leading to an open plaza and a large medieval-style church. She hugged herself as she wondered what today would bring. Hearing the door open behind her, she turned. Laken entered the sitting room from the bedroom, fully dressed in a pair of khaki pants and a black t-shirt, but no socks or shoes. His hair was still damp from the shower. Her hands itched to go over and run through it.

"I ordered breakfast from room service. It should be here anytime. I didn't know what you liked, so it's a little of everything," Laken said. "You should have time to take a quick shower and dress."

Harper replied, "Thank you. I'll do that." She hurried through getting ready, realizing how hungry she was after not eating much the night before. Harper wore a gray camo print t-shirt dress and a soft pink long-sleeved cardigan. She also opted for no shoes, since it seemed they wouldn't yet be ready to leave for a bit, then headed out to join Laken for break-fast.

Laken was just finishing with the room service serv-er when Harper joined him. He pulled out the chair for her to sit, then offered her a choice of coffee, tea, or orange juice. Choosing coffee, Harper looked at the spread of food in front of her and laughed. "You really ordered a little of everything, didn't you?" she asked.

Looking a little sheepish, Laken replied, "Yes. I didn't want to wake you up to ask what you would like. Eat, and then once you're done, we'll head to my house. Your items are due to arrive from Boston later this afternoon. It would be good for you to do a walkthrough so you can decide where you want to put your things."

The two of them finished the rest of breakfast in silence before packing their overnight bags. They headed to the front desk where Laken did the checkout, then to the parking garage. Laken had arranged earlier for his car to be dropped off. He took Harper's overnight bag and put both in the car's trunk before opening the door for her.

Harper turned to look at Laken during the drive back. She said to him, "What did Michael mean at dinner that night when he said that he was leaving all his money to me and you didn't need any of it?"

Glancing over at her, Laken replied, "I'm the CEO and president of Wolffang Enterprises. I've no need of money, and he wants to make sure that you have your own. Though I've set up a monthly allowance for you already. I don't plan for my wife to lack anything. Your card should arrive in the next couple of days, and you just need to let me know if there is anything else that you need."

"Wolffang Enterprises? Wow! I think most homes in the US have a piece of your technology in them. I heard that Wolffang Enterprises began only nine years ago. If I remember correctly, Michael said you were only a year older than him, so that makes you 28 years old?"

"Yes, I started the company in my first year of college. I studied electrical engineering, and by the time I graduated with my Bachelor's degree, I was a millionaire. Later, I got my Master's degree in business." Laken further explained.

"What about you?" asked Laken. "I only know the little Michael has mentioned about you and what the two of you discussed at dinner that night. Which is honestly not much."

Harper smiled. "That isn't much, is it? Michael and I grew up in Boston. He's older than I am by five years, and my mother married his father when he was two years old. Michael moved to California to go to college, and that's when he met you, I believe. I graduated with my Bachelor's degree in History from Northeastern University and had just started my Master's degree at Harvard when all this started. My focus areas are medieval texts and the occult, specifically werewolves."

Enzo growled in his head, *What?!*

Laken started and pressed his foot on the brake forcefully, causing the car and both of them to jolt forward.

"What?!" Harper exclaimed.

"Sorry," said Laken, thinking quickly. "A squirrel ran into the road."

Harper looked back and forth in front of the car. "Really? I saw nothing."

"Tell me more about your Master's," replied Laken as he continued driving.

"Most of my thesis entails finding and translating medieval texts that prove that werewolves really existed," explained Harper.

Laken asked, "You don't strike me as a werewolf enthusiast. How did this become such a passion of yours that you made it a focus of your Master's?"

"When I was a child, my parents read me tons of fairy tales and folklore. I grew to love mythology, paranormal, and fantasy books. *Hunchback of Notre Dame*, *Dracula*, and *The Werewolf of Paris* were some of my favorite books. Going into history never seemed to be a question. In my Historical Literature course, we discussed the origins of fairy tales and their basis in historical accuracy. It made me look into some of my favorite stories, and I found that most research related to werewolves."

Laken pulled up to the gate of his house in the Marina District and pushed in the code on the keypad. While they waited for the gate to open, he wondered about the news of Harper's thesis. He would need to monitor this if she continued working on it. If her research threatened exposing the world of werewolves, he would need to intervene. It could also affect how she would accept his being a werewolf. Historical accounts weren't accurate nor nice towards his kind.

Harper could see the Golden Gate Bridge past the house and the water of the bay. She couldn't believe that she would live in a house that was right on the water. Plus, the size of the house was immense. She had thought Michael's house was big, but this place was much bigger.

Pulling the car through the gate, Laken pulled up to the door and parked. He got out, then opened the door and helped Harper out of the car. Next, he took the overnight bags from the trunk. Pointing to the garage to the left of the house, he said, "I've two other cars in the garage. You're welcome to take either of them when you want to go somewhere. The keys hang inside the garage. We'll set up your own codes for the gate and the house."

Laken turned to the house and punched in a code on the keypad next to the front door to unlock it and disable the alarm system. He set the overnight bags just inside the door, then turned to Harper. He swung her up into his arms as Harper gave a little yelp. Laken smiled and said, "Just following tradition." He stepped over the threshold of the house and set Harper down in the foyer. "Let me show you around." He continued to hold her hand and glanced down to where the mate bond wrapped around their wrists.

Harper looked around at Laken's house. It was two stories with a sweeping staircase that went to the second floor on each side, with the foyer in the center that went all the way to patio doors that led to the backyard. On the right side were a family room, half bath, and a study. To the left was a dining room and kitchen. While the house was grand, it was not ostentatious. Harper found the downstairs had a pleasant flow and was modern, yet homey. The study had books on a shelf that she couldn't wait to explore while sitting in the comfortable chairs. The family room seemed more formal, and the dining room table was large enough to seat ten, but it didn't give off an oppressive feeling if only the two of them sat at it to eat.

Laken led her through each room before heading up the right-side staircase to show her the upstairs. She found it comforting that he held her hand while he led her around his home. The second level consisted of two guest rooms, each with its own bathroom, an office, and a master bedroom suite. Harper noticed that there were no family photos in the house, which she planned to ask about and remedy when her things arrived. She enjoyed that there was plenty of artwork to break up the wall space in the home.

He explained, "I have regular staff, but I gave them the day off today. I didn't want to overwhelm you. There is a housekeeper, groundskeeper, and chef. The chef left us lunch and dinner, something easy to warm up and serve ourselves."

Harper hesitated at the main suite's door. Laken took her hand and pulled her in. The suite was enormous, as large as some people's apartments. It had a sitting area with a fireplace, a changing room connected to a his/her closet, a bathroom with both shower and jacuzzi tub, as well as a king-size bed. There was also a set of double doors that led out to a balcony that connected the suite to the office.

Laken took Harper's hands in his. "My promise stands, but this is our room. We'll share it and the bed just as we did last night."

Harper looked down and away from Laken. He took her chin and turned her face back up to his, and lightly kissed her. "Please don't be afraid of me, of this."

"Laken, it's not that. It's just that I've never been in a relationship this serious. What I'm feeling..." Harper trailed off.

Laken smiled down at Harper. "I understand. What I feel for you is new to me, too. Why don't we go have some lunch before the moving truck arrives? I still need to show you the backyard, too."

Heading back downstairs, Laken led Harper through the main foyer to a set of double doors. These opened onto a large patio overlooking a pool and sweeping lawn. The lawn went right up to the fenced beach area on the bay. Harper couldn't contain her excitement at having access to both a pool and the beach. She gasped and laughed, then turned to hug Laken without thinking.

"This is great! I've always wanted a pool," Harper exclaimed. She then realized she was still hugging Laken and stepped back.

Laken smiled down at her as he let her go. He was pleased that he had made her happy. "I'm glad you like it. It's heated so that you can use it any time of the year. We can use it later or tomorrow. Let's go eat now."

After lunch, the moving truck arrived, and they spent the rest of the afternoon unloading Harper's belongings, working with the movers to unpack, and directing them on where to put everything. Dinner was late, and they both fell into bed exhausted.

Chapter 5

THE next day, Harper woke up to find herself in bed alone. She took a shower, dressed, and headed downstairs. She found Laken in the study and overheard him on the phone telling someone to cancel his appointments for the next couple of days, as he would stay home to spend time with her. As she walked into the study, Laken hung up the phone and looked up to see her there. His face lit up with a smile, and he stood up. "Good morning! Are you ready for breakfast?"

In the dining room, a continental spread awaited them. Laken let her know that if she wanted anything made, she just needed to let the chef know. He took her into the kitchen to introduce her to him. The chef, professionally trained in New York, prided himself on meeting Laken and her needs. He wore a black chef's hat and apron to work every day.

After they ate, Laken called in the housekeeper and groundskeeper so Harper could meet them. Mrs. Redmoon was the housekeeper's name, and Harper loved her immediately. Laken explained that the woman had been working for him since he had bought the house four years before. She was in her 50s with a full head of silver-gray hair that was styled in curls. She wore the traditional black house-keeper dress with a white apron over it and black orthopedic shoes. Laken told Harper that he had told Mrs. Redmoon she could wear whatever she wanted, and this was what she chose.

Harper found the groundskeeper to be a quiet fel-low with whom she would rarely interact. He took care of all the yardwork, as well as the upkeep of the pool, beach, and the cars.

After the introductions were complete, Laken asked if there was anywhere in San Francisco she wanted to go. He wanted to take her on a tour of the town she now lived in and show her around. The two picked out places together to visit and made an itinerary. It was quickly apparent that it would take more than a day to go everywhere on their list.

Laken spent the following two days taking Harper to see both the famous and lesser-known landmarks of San Francisco. They rode the cable cars, strolled along Fisherman's Wharf, visited the Cable Car Museum, toured Alcatraz Island, and walked through Golden Gate Park. They ate at Ghirardelli Square, Hook Fish Co, and had breakfast with Irish Coffee at The Buena Vista. During their eating, drinking, and touring, they learned about each other: how they grew up, their likes and dislikes, and dreams.

Harper found herself more comfortable with Laken, but also craving his touch. She enjoyed it when he took her hand, when they walked from place to place and leaned into him when they sat next to each other. Of the places they visited, her favorite was Golden Gate Park. She still missed Boston, but getting to know San Francisco was helping her to like it more. There were similarities between the two places that helped with her assimilation as well.

During their time sightseeing, Harper and Laken also took time to get to know each other better. While Laken asked Harper about her time growing up, she noticed he didn't talk about his parents or childhood. This, besides the lack of family photos, initially made her wary of asking him about it. She gathered up courage on their second day out to ask him.

"Laken, can I ask you a question?" asked Harper as they had lunch after touring Alcatraz Island.

Laken looked at Harper questioningly. They had talked so much; he wondered what she wanted to ask that she felt the need to request permission first. "Of course."

"I noticed that you have no family photos in the house, and you also never talk about your past before college. May I ask what happened to your parents? Do you have any family alive?" Harper asked, though she looked at her plate the whole time, moving her food around with her fork.

It had been a long time since anyone had asked Laken about his family. His pack knew his history and why he never spoke about it. Michael had been told that his parents were dead and that he was an only child. They had discussed it so many years ago that they no longer brought up the topic.

Reaching out to touch Harper's hand and catch her attention, Laken apologized, "Harper, I'm sorry for not sharing that part of my life with you. I didn't do so in avoidance or on purpose. I've been on my own for so long that it's just an accepted part of my life."

Harper looked up at Laken's touch, and her face took on a look of surprise at his words.

"My parents died when I was twelve years old, and I was, am an only child. As far as I know, I've no direct relatives. I've been on my own since my parents died, and I have no photos of my family. Every day I wish I had photos of my parents and of us as a family, but it's something I just don't have." Laken continued.

Reaching out to take his hands, Harper folded his within her own. Silent tears ran down her face. As her own parents were gone, she knew what that was like, but she at least had had Michael. She couldn't imagine being completely alone in the world at such a young age.

Laken squeezed her hands. "I think my background is another reason Michael wanted me to marry you. I cherish my friends like my family. And now I have you; you're my family as well. We'll have one of our wedding photos printed and put up at the house, as well as photos of you, me, and Michael. How does that sound?" Harper smiled and nodded her consent to his question.

Laken also enjoyed their excursions. He held Harper's hand, put his arm over her shoulder, hugged her to his side, or touched her in any other way he could, sneaking it as much as she would allow. Every time he held her hand, the mate bond would weave itself around their wrists, filling both him and Enzo with joy at having their mate by their side. He and Harper were growing closer, which was what he had hoped.

They had even enjoyed a couple of kisses, one even as deep as the one at their wedding. This had occurred after dinner at Ghirardelli Square. They had finished the evening off by looking at the shops in the Square before strolling down by the water. While the sun was setting, they sat on a bench and shared their favorites. The wind had kicked up and blew Harper's hair across her face. Laken then reached out a hand to brush it back behind her ear. When he did this, he had leaned forward, and it had seemed natural to kiss her. That kiss had escalated, and they had broken apart with both of them breathless, when a bicycle had ridden past.

Each day of their outings, they arrived home happy but exhausted. They fell into bed, both sleeping soundly. The mornings were another story for Laken. As with the morning after the wedding, he woke to find Harper lying against him. He would have to entangle himself, calm his wolf, and take a cold shower to prevent frightening her.

On the fourth day of their marriage, Harper came down after her shower to find Laken in the study, finishing up a phone call. "Good morning," she said.

Laken turned around in the chair, looking at Harper. "Good morning to you. What're your plans for today? I have to go to the office. With it being Friday and my having been off for four days, there are things to take care of before the weekend."

"Well, I'd like to see if there is a university in town where I can continue my Master's. So, I think I'll plan on doing research into that. I need to set up my desk and organize it in the office," replied Harper. "Since I haven't yet used the pool, I was thinking of going swimming. I may also see what Michael is up to. I was thinking of inviting him over for dinner. If it's okay with you, that is."

Laken smiled. "Yes, it would be great to have dinner with him. Why don't you call him and then let the chef know if there'll be an extra person for dinner?" Standing up, Laken kissed Harper on the cheek. "I have to head out now. See you later."

The difference in Michael's appearance from four days earlier shocked Harper and Laken. He had lost weight, was pale, and walked in with the help of a cane. Harper rushed over to help him.

Michael waved her off. "I'm fine, Harper."

"Just let me walk next to you. It'll make me feel better," said Harper.

"Okay, okay." Michael gave in.

Dinner was a solemn affair, with Laken and Harper watching as Michael picked over his plate of food. They both tried to be upbeat, talking about the previous days they had spent together. Michael smiled as he listened to their tales. His assurance of Harper's future was obvious in his relaxed demeanor, despite his discomfort from the toll of the tumor ravaging his body.

After saying goodbye to Michael, they walked to the sitting room at the end of the night. They shared their concerns about Michael over glasses of wine. Later, in bed, Harper sobbed and turned to Laken. She pleaded with him, "Please hold me, Laken." Laken wrapped her in his arms, and they fell asleep that way.

The next day, Laken took time after breakfast to work from home, even though it was Saturday. He still had important paperwork that he needed to catch up on, but he didn't need to go into the office to do it. Harper was still down after seeing Michael the night before. She sat out on the balcony of their bedroom, attempting to read a book on werewolf history for her thesis. After two hours of flipping pages but not really absorbing anything significant, she gave up and went looking for Laken.

She didn't find him in the office as she expected, but in the kitchen. Laken was talking to the chef, and they both turned to her, stunned, when she entered the room.

"Well, there goes the surprise," said Laken.

Harper asked, "Surprise?"

"Yes, I was having the chef set up a picnic lunch on the pool patio. I remember you saying you had yet to use the pool yesterday, and I wasn't sure if you had had the chance. I figured we could sit out there, eat a light picnic lunch, and swim. It's such a nice day out, and there is no guarantee how long the beautiful weather will hold out. Soon fall will be upon us." Laken gestured towards the back of the house while he talked.

Harper smiled, realizing Laken had tried to plan a surprise for her, and she had interrupted it. "I never swam yesterday. The other tasks I had to do took longer than I had expected, and then it was time for dinner with Michael." The last made her voice trail off.

Laken hurried to bring her thoughts back to the swim. His goal with the picnic and pool was to keep her from thinking about Michael. "Why don't we go change while the picnic gets set up, then? You go ahead while I finish up the last few details?"

The smile returned to Harper's face, and she nodded while turning to the door to head upstairs. Laken quickly finished talking to the chef, then followed behind her. By the time he had made it to the bedroom, Harper had changed. She had on a swim cover, so Laken didn't see what kind of swimsuit she had on. He reminded her that towels were by the pool, so he would be down behind her.

Laken found Harper already snacking on the picnic lunch when he arrived on the patio. He joined her in eating first, then they lay on the loungers afterward for a while, talking about plans for the week.

After a while, Harper sat up and pulled off the swim cover, revealing a two-piece bikini comprising a halter top and a high-waist bottom. It was modest by bikini standards, but the style fit Harper perfectly. Laken sucked in a breath at seeing the most of his wife thus far in their marriage. It showed off her high, full breasts, as well as her slightly rounded stomach, curvaceous hips, and sculpted legs. While petite, Harper's body was proportionate. She wasn't super skinny, nor was she overweight. Instead, she was trim yet curvy where she needed to be.

Harper noticed Laken looking at her and raised her eyebrows questioningly. He shook his head at her in response to show nothing. She grinned back and turned to enter the pool. Taking a break, Laken decided he would need a minute before following her in to take control of his body. He watched her dive under the water, then surface, tip her head back, and smooth her hair away from her face. Okay, maybe more than a minute.

Harper swam lazily around the pool. It was the perfect temperature, both the water and the weather. She wondered when Laken was going to join her and had turned to ask him when he stood up. He took off the t-shirt he had worn down from the room, and Harper gulped upon seeing his bare chest. Laken had worn full pajamas to bed since the night of their wedding. She thought it was to make her more comfortable. Seeing him now, she was happy he had — otherwise, she may have been too distracted to sleep. She wanted to rub her hands across his chest and feel whether the hair on it was soft or wiry. Harper turned away quickly as she realized she was staring.

She heard Laken enter the pool and swim towards her. Paddling lightly away, she pretended she hadn't been looking his way and had just noticed him. Once he was close, she splashed him. He acted shocked and splashed her back. This started a water fight with the two of them acting like children for a bit, splashing and laughing.

Finally, after chasing Harper across the pool, Laken caught and caged her with his hands, holding on to either side of the edge. They were both laughing with the fun of the water fight, but when Harper put her hand on Laken's chest to stop the water from pushing him into her, his face quickly changed from humor to shock to need, and his laughter stopped. She hadn't seen this change initially, as she had been looking at where her hand was, but once she looked at his face to see why he was quiet, she stopped laughing as well.

"Laken?" she asked.

One of Laken's hands let go of the edge and reached down, then around her back to pull her closer. His other hand entangled in her hand as he leaned down to kiss her. Harper gasped as his lips pressed against hers. This was not like the other kisses they had shared thus far. It was full of hunger. Soon his tongue pressed against the seam of her mouth, asking and demanding entrance at the same time.

With a moan, Harper opened, and their tongues twined, twisted, and engaged in a dance that only they knew the steps to.

Harper slid the hand that was still on Laken's chest upwards as her other hand joined to wrap around his neck and pulled him closer. Simultaneously, Laken's hands slid down Harper's body to grab her hips and pull hers to his. While still a virgin, there was no mistaking the firm proof of desire for her that was pressed against her core. Deepening the kiss, Harper lifted her legs and wrapped them around Laken's hips, locking her ankles at the small of his back. It was his turn to groan as he moved them the short distance backwards to the wall of the pool.

With the wall supporting Harper, Laken moved his hands to her head to move his mouth to her neck. He had just nuzzled at her neck when Enzo breathed in his head, Mark her.

Realizing he was on the edge of losing control, Laken pulled back to take a deep breath. It was then that he saw Harper, and that was almost enough to cause his downfall. With her head thrown back, eyes closed, and lips parted, she breathed as uncontrollably as he. She also chose that moment to twist her hips against his in need.

Raising a hand, Laken slid it slowly down her face from her hairline to her collarbone when he had to stop himself. With the light touch, Harper opened her eyes, though they were slightly unfocused.

"That was unexpected, but delightful. However, I think the pool may not be the place for us to get carried away." Laken said with a grin.

His words caused a blush to spread across Harper's face. She let her legs slide down from his torso, but Laken grabbed them to hold them in place. He didn't want her to feel embarrassed or regret what had happened between them. The two of them had been getting comfortable with each other, and Laken knew he was slowly falling in love with Harper.

"Where do you think you're going? I don't want you to think that this was something wrong or to regret anything. Obviously, I want you." Laken stopped and kissed her again for effect, and pressed his hips to hers. "I would love to continue this; I just meant that, where this is heading, the pool is not the place for it."

Shyly, Harper answered, "I feel the same. I mean, I want you too. But I'm not sure if I'm ready yet. We've only known each other for a handful of days."

"I understand. I've said that I would wait, and I will. When you're ready," Laken promised.

Chapter 6

THREE days later, Michael died. Harper was inconsolable. She spent the first day crying in bed. The second day she spent in the chair in their room staring at the fire. Laken had to beg her to eat something both days. His own grief had to take a backseat to caring for his wife.

Michael's memorial service was two days after his death. It rained that day, as if the world was also crying for the life taken too early. Michael had pre-planned his cremation and memorial service, so there was nothing for Harper and Laken to do but attend. Harper sat and accepted sympathy from those who attended, but didn't recall who actually spoke with her. She was relieved when it was over and she could return to the house.

Someone handed Harper the urn containing Michael's ashes. She hugged it tight and almost broke down again. Laken put his arm around her shoulder and led her out to the car.

Laken and Harper both sat at the dining table, picking at their dinner. Neither had much of an appetite after the emotional day. They had each nibbled on the appetizers that had been at the memorial service, and that seemed to have been enough for the meager amount of food they needed.

They had placed the urn on the mantle in the study. Laken had told Harper that it had been Michael's favorite place when he visited the house. They would go to Boston next week to inter his ashes per his last wishes.

Harper finally pushed the chair back and excused herself. "I'm heading upstairs."

Laken watched her leave and stopped pretending to eat his own food. Forgetting all etiquette, he pushed his plate away and rested his head on the palms of his hands with his elbows braced on the table. He had tried to get close to his wife and mate, only to feel like he was back to square one after Michael's death. He was grieving too, but not sure she even realized it. Now he was just too tired to think about it.

He walked up the stairs and opened the door to the bedroom, shutting it softly behind him. Turning, he saw Harper sitting on the edge of the bed, facing away from him. She hunched over in the most despondent posture he had ever seen. He pivoted away from the sight and slipped into the dressing room to change into his pajamas.

Sitting on the bench, he took off his shoes and socks, tossing the socks into the hamper, then placing the shoes under the bureau. Next, he unbuttoned his shirt and balled it up before also throwing that into the hamper. He was stunned when Harper's hands and then her cheek pressed against his back. He hadn't heard her walk into the dressing room.

"Thank you for supporting me these last few days. I know you've been grieving too but have set it aside for me," she said, running her hands down his back, around his sides, and sliding them around his middle.

Laken put his hands over hers. He turned in her arms so he was facing Harper. "Michael was my friend, but he was your brother. I can only imagine what you have been going through."

"I want to pay you back for everything you have done," continued Harper. She slid her hands around to his front and flattened her hands to his chest as she pressed herself against him.

Laken tipped his head back and clenched his hands into fists, straining to resist, while Enzo encouraged him to take what she offered. He had been so patient every night and morning when she lay next to him. "You don't have to do this, moonflower. I don't want you to regret anything."

"I'm also tired of fighting this thing between us." Harper licked her lips, glancing up at him through her lashes while she rubbed her hands up and down his muscles.

Looking down at Harper's face, Laken smashed his mouth to hers, swallowing her moan. Her arms wrapped around his neck, and he reached down to pull her hips against his. He felt her press her lips harder against his as well as rock her hips forward, which caused him to groan.

"Please, Laken. Tonight, I need to feel," Harper pleaded as they pulled apart for a breath. She slid one hand down and pressed it to the erection that was straining against his pants.

"Damn it," he swore softly.

Harper opened her mouth to his when she felt his tongue probing at her lips. She ran her fingers through his hair as the kiss deepened. Laken turned and pressed her back against the dressing room wall, then lifted her so she could wrap her legs around his waist. She gasped as the movement pressed her core against his straining hardness.

Laken carried her to the bedroom and set her down next to the bed. He brushed her hair away from her face and slid the robe off her shoulders until it fell to the floor. He asked once more, "Are you sure? Once I start, there is no way I'll be able to stop."

Her answer was to reach out, kiss his neck, then unbuckle his belt, pull it out of the loops and toss it aside. She kissed her way across his chest as she undid the button and zipper of his pants. He kicked them off his legs and out of the way after sliding them down.

Laken touched her shoulder where the strap of her negligee had slid off. He did the same to the other strap, and this caused the slopes of her breasts to be bare as the top caught on her straining nipples. Leaning over, he followed the curves with the knuckle of one hand, then his lips followed the same course.

Harper let her arms straighten to her sides, and the negligee fell to the floor, leaving her naked to his gaze. Sliding his hands down her arms, Laken dropped to his knees in front of Harper and pulled her to him. He pulled a nipple into his mouth while a hand caressed the other breast. His other arm went around her back to help hold her upright.

Moaning at the sensations rushing through her, Harper wove her fingers through his hair. Her other hand grabbed his shoulder and held on as she felt as though the floor was moving under her. She felt a rush of moisture between her legs. She had been wet before, but not like this.

Laken moved his mouth to the other breast to give it the same attention. His other hand slid down her ribs and onto her inner thigh. He reached to test her core and found her wet and ready. He groaned against her nipple.

Scooping her up, he placed her in the center of their bed, then stepped back to remove his briefs. He moved back to join her on the bed, and Harper reached out a hand to touch him. Laken stopped her, and she looked at him questioningly.

"If you touch me, this party is going to be over before it starts," he said with a cocked eyebrow.

Harper opened her eyes wide. Laken took both her hands and pulled them over her head. He told her, "Pull your knees up, moonflower."

She did as he asked, and he kissed her as he slowly pushed himself inside her, her hymen breaking with a brief pain. She moaned, feeling herself stretch to accommodate his hardness. Laken continued to push forward, then let her hands go and moved his mouth to her nipple again. Harper grabbed his shoulder, and her nails dug in as he fully seated himself inside her wet warmth.

He lifted his head to ask, "Are you okay?" His breaths were coming in the same quick spurts as hers.

Harper grabbed his face with both hands to kiss him deeply, bite his lower lip, and then reply, "Yes!"

With that response, Laken let go and plunged in and out of her. Harper flung her head back, wrapped her ankles around his hips, and grabbed his buttocks with her nails.

"Please, Laken!" she cried.

At that, Laken reached down to hold her hips and adjust the angle of his penetration. He bent his head and bit a nipple lightly. Harper felt the spasms inside start and cried out as she stiffened and climaxed. She barely heard as Laken yelled out, "Moon Goddess, yes, Harper!" as he thrust inside her three more times before falling on top of her.

A short time later, Harper felt Laken leave the bed, then return. She turned her head, and he had a warm washcloth in his hand. "Do you want to do it, or should I?" he asked.

She blushed and replied, "I can. Thank you." Taking the washcloth, she cleaned herself, briefly noticing the small spot of red from losing her virginity. Laken took care of the washcloth, then climbed back into bed, pulling her against him as they fell asleep.

The following morning, Harper woke to an erotic dream happening in real life. Laken had her half turned on her back while he lay next to her on his side. He was sucking her breast while his hand was rubbing her sensitive nub. She was already wet and panting upon waking. Just as she realized what was going on, he slid in her from behind, eliciting a groan from them both.

Laken lifted his head to look at her with a wicked grin on his face. "Oh, you're awake?"

With him continuing to tease her between her legs with his fingers and stroke his length in and out of her, she could barely think, let alone answer. She moaned in response and closed her eyes as he kissed her throat and her orgasm took her over.

Laken was moments behind her. She turned her head to look at him, and he kissed her gently before pecking her on the nose. He slid out of her, then handed her some tissues from next to the bed. "Let's go shower. I know you have plans today, and I need to go to the office."

Harper had to meet with Michael's lawyer to go over his will. She sat down and told the man, "Let's get started, please. I know Michael left everything to me, so where do I sign? I just want to get this over with."

The lawyer set a stack of papers in front of her. "These are the documents regarding the valuation and transfer of the MD Group to Mr. Howlkind. Mr. Deveraugh set up an account in your name at the Bank of San Francisco and deposited the entire sale of the business there. I need you to initial at the bottom of the first three pages, then sign on the last page, please."

Harper signed the pages, reviewing nothing. However, on the last page, a figure made her pause. "Wait, what amount did they deposit into my account?" She asked.

"Well, this is how much the business sold for, plus what Michael had in his personal bank accounts. The federal inheritance tax of 3% reduced the amount to $2,182,500, which we deposited," the lawyer explained. "His personal effects have yet to be evaluated, auctioned, and sold."

"You're saying I'm a millionaire?" Harper exclaimed.

The lawyer looked at her in surprise. "Why, yes. Didn't Mr. Deveraugh tell you how much he was leaving to you?"

Harper shook her head. "No, he didn't." *Why didn't you tell me, Michael?*

After their parents' death, Michael and Harper had each inherited a small amount, but nothing substantial. They had sold the house and split the money. She had used it to pay the rent for the apartment she had stayed at while in college, then to help pay for tuition and not take out an exorbitant amount of student loans.

"Here are your account card and debit card. Next, I need you to determine what personal items you want to keep from Mr. Deveraugh's estate. Once you have, I can arrange for the estate sales agent to come in to set up the auction and then sell his house and car. I know he has already been out to the house to do an initial walkthrough. After these steps, we can deposit the proceeds from the personal sales. I've estimated those to be another $1,750,000," the lawyer concluded.

"Well, thank you for everything. I'll go to the house this weekend and let you know on Monday that you can proceed." Shocked, Harper looked at her hands. Michael truly had left her well off.

Chapter 7

HARPER asked Laken to go with her to Michael's house to look through it after lunch on Saturday. She thought there might be items there that he would want as well. He had been Michael's best friend and had known him for almost eight years. She had set aside most of both Saturday and Sunday to do this necessary but difficult task.

The estate sales agent had already been to the house twice and set aside several items that he had identified that she would want. There were photo albums, jewelry, watches, and a stack of art.

Laken touched her on the shoulder and let her know he was going to go do his own walkthrough. She nodded in assent, and he kissed her before he left. Harper didn't know where to start. She had only been in Michael's home a few times and wasn't completely familiar with the house.

Harper looked up as Laken returned with a couple of ties and a hat in his hand to find Harper still standing where he had left her. "Is there something wrong?" he asked.

"I don't know where to look for anything," she admitted.

Laken asked, "Besides the things that are already out there, what else do you want to look for? Or what rooms do you want to look through? I can help you."

Taking her hand, he pulled her forward and led her up the stairs to Michael's home office. "Let's start here."

Laken led her room by room through Michael's house for several hours until almost dinnertime. They had made headway, but came back the next day to finish. He also said that he would call people to come get the items first thing Monday morning and deliver them to the house.

On Sunday, it was easier and faster to finish going through the rest of the house. They were completed by lunchtime and ate before heading back. Laken took Harper to Scoma's Restaurant. Well known in the area, he also thought it would be reminiscent of her Boston roots with its seafood options.

Harper truly enjoyed the food and the time they spent together during their lunch. Afterwards, Laken asked her to walk with him along the wharf. He held her hand, and they spoke of Michael. The memories didn't hurt as much. At the end of the afternoon, Laken said, "Let's go home." Harper realized she was thinking of his place as her home now.

She recalled last night and his calling her "moonflower." Did that mean he had feelings for her?

Monday, Harper decided she needed to get her California driver's license, and name change completed. She didn't realize that it would take most of the day.

She started out at the City Hall with her marriage license and birth certificate in hand. With that finally done, she had to go to the Social Security office next to get that changed. Last was the California DMV with her temporary name change paperwork and her Massachusetts driver's license.

Five hours later, she realized after all this that the bank with her account would need this new information, so she was off for one more stop. At least that was a quick one, as they only needed to look at her paperwork to adjust the name there.

Arriving at the house, she was looking at her new ID with the name Harper Howlkind as she entered to find all the items from Michael's house had arrived. Harper realized that she and Laken hadn't decided on where they would put the art. She took the photo albums up to their shared office space and placed them with the others she had seen on the bookshelves there. Harper wiped her forehead, and she returned downstairs. She was feeling flushed and warm. She took off the cardigan she was wearing. There were a few other items to be placed in the sitting room, so she took care of those and placed the art in the study. She collected the jewelry, watches, ties, and other items that should go into the bedroom with her there.

Upstairs, Harper put the items on top of the bureau in the dressing room. She still felt flushed and was warmer than before. Maybe she should take her temperature and a lukewarm shower. She hadn't been sick in a long time and had never been prone to illnesses. However, what she really felt was needy and turned on sexually. This was definitely not something she had ever experienced before.

It had been a busy day. Laken had started by calling in a favor to have the items from Michael's house picked up and brought over to his house. He had also bought the tickets for their trip to Boston this weekend, besides the other items on his daily agenda. He rolled his neck to stretch the muscles as he climbed the stairs to go see where his wife was.

Laken opened the door to the bedroom, and one sniff made him harden and Enzo howl in his head. How could Harper smell like a she-wolf in heat? Was it because of the mate bond? But that made little sense. She-wolves went into heat twice a year, and it was when they could conceive a pup. He didn't think that a human would change reproductively because of being mated with a werewolf. Or was he more sensitive to Harper's "time of the month" because he was her mate? It still didn't explain why her scent had changed from this morning. However, Laken also couldn't say that he was an expert. He wondered whether anyone had even conducted any research on this.

He could hear the shower running and shed his clothes on his way to the bathroom. Upon entering, he gave thanks for the open-concept design that gave him a direct view of his wife. Harper stood under the spray, cupping her breasts, not having noticed him yet. If he hadn't yet been as hard as a rock, he would have been so seeing her. She turned, bracing her hands against the wall and widening her stance.

Laken stepped into the shower stall, wrapped his hands around her middle, and pulled her back against him. He realized the water was tepid, as Harper had been trying to cool her overheated body. She gasped in shock at his sudden presence, then moaned as one hand slid down to cup her mound and the other took a breast as his mouth kissed across her shoulder.

Harper's head dropped back onto his shoulder. Then he rubbed himself against her core. She reached back to grab his hair with her hand while the other grabbed the back of his thigh to pull him closer.

Laken pressed his mouth to her neck and opened his mouth before he even realized what he was do-ing. *Mark her!* Enzo yelled. He pulled his head back and took several deep breaths. He couldn't believe he had almost lost complete control.

Turning Harper around, Laken took a few steps back to sit on the tiled shower's built-in seat. He pulled her down onto his lap and slid into her all in one move. Laken swallowed Harper's moan with his kiss. He wrapped one arm around her back and held her hip with his hand to guide her movements. He released her mouth to groan as Harper ground her hips to his.

Harper grabbed his shoulders, and he hissed, feeling her nails dig in. He smiled despite the slight pain. He adjusted her position so her heated center would rub against the base of his hardness. Doing so started ripples in her sheath that surrounded him.

Laken felt the ripples become stronger, squeezing him. He grabbed Harper's hips and bucked into her while she ground onto him. Laken yelled his release while Harper was equally vociferous with hers. He held her as she melted into his arms in the aftermath.

I've never experienced sex like this before. Laken thought. *That's because it's not just sex, it's mating*, Enzo replied.

Using voice commands, Laken turned off the water and lifted Harper, carrying her out of the shower. He brought her to the bed and laid her down. Harper protested she would get the bed wet. Returning to the bedroom, Laken had wrapped a towel around his waist and brought a towel for Harper. He sat her up and helped her to dry off, then tucked her into bed before drying himself and joining her in bed.

"What about dinner?" Harper asked.

Laken growled, "I think I'll have you."

Harper squealed as he dove under the covers; then, for a while, only her moans were audible.

Laken met with Jora in his office at Wolffang Enterprises. He needed to get some answers about what had happened with Harper two days before. If anyone would have an idea about relationships, it would be Jora, as she had been a healer in her previous pack. She had also studied human medicine as a midwife when she had moved to San Francisco.

Jora explained to him that it did indeed sound like Harper had experienced enhanced ovulation. She had never heard of it, but also said she hadn't read or heard of research on human females mated with werewolves. His Alpha status could also have been a factor. That was an even rarer mating than just a regular werewolf mating with a human.

She said that he could connect with her for advice again or send Harper to her for a consultation. Laken thanked the Elder for taking the time to meet with him. He had received no actual answers, but had more questions.

That Friday, they took the late flight to Boston. They would take care of Michael's last request for his ashes. At their last dinner together, Michael had explained to Harper that when he had ordered the headstone for their parents, he had it specially made. It had storage spots at each end for cremation remains for each of them. She had wondered why it had plain places on the front, as if it still had spots for more engraving. It turns out that was exactly what it was for.

A couple of days before leaving for Boston, Harper had called the engraving company and given them all the information for the addition to the headstone. Before their flight, a company representative phoned Harper to announce the engraving's completion.

Upon arrival, Laken and Harper checked into their hotel, placed their carry-on bags in the room, and then had a late light dinner at the bar that was still open. "What time are we to be at the cemetery?" asked Laken.

Harper looked up from her food. "Ummm, 10:30 am."

"Well, since it's almost 11, let's head up to bed," said Laken, looking at his watch and getting up to throw away their trash.

"Sounds good to me," replied Harper.

Up in the room, Harper finished washing up and left the bathroom to find Laken in bed, waiting for her. He lifted the covers for her, showing he was naked. She lifted an eyebrow.

"I'm too tired for anything tonight, but I won't deny myself the feeling of your body next to mine, either," he said.

Harper shed her clothes and slid in next to him. He covered them both, pulled her close to him, and they both drifted off.

The next day, Laken awoke and looked at his wife sleeping. He gently traced a finger over her lips. They had been married for three weeks now, and he couldn't imagine his life without her in it. He could see why a mate made a werewolf happy. Laken knew he loved her with all he was, too. He wondered if she loved him, even a little.

He smiled as he watched her eyes flutter open. "Good morning."

Harper smiled back. "Good morning to you."

Laken pressed his lips to hers and drank in the taste of her. He grinned with his mouth still on hers. "We need to get moving. It's already after 8."

"Really?" exclaimed Harper, leaning to the side to glance at the clock. She couldn't believe they had slept so late. They had less than two hours to dress, eat, and get to the cemetery.

Laken said, "I'll order room service while you take a shower. While I would love to take advantage of your lack of clothes, we have more important things to do right now. What would you like?"

An hour later, the two had showered, dressed, and were sitting down to eat their room service breakfast. Laken let her know he had also set up a taxi to arrive at 10 to pick them up. The cemetery was a twenty-minute drive away.

During the ride to the cemetery, Laken held Harper's hand. She cradled the urn with Michael's ashes with her other arm. Her head rested on his shoulder, and both were quiet with their own thoughts.

Upon arrival, Laken directed the driver to the spot where he could see the cemetery sexton was waiting for them. Asking the taxi to wait, they joined the sexton at the plot. Laken pulled the keys that Michael had provided from his pocket. The sexton used a spade to pull back the grass from the side of the headstone, revealing the keyhole. Handing over the keys, the sexton opened the hidden side container and pulled it out.

Harper kissed the container holding Michael's remains, then handed it over. The sexton carefully fitted it into the container before replacing it and locking it back in place. They held hands, then moved around to the front of the headstone to view the new engraving of Michael's resting place. Harper rested her head on Laken's chest, and he let go of her hand to wrap his arm around her shoulders. They stood there in silent reflection. The sexton quietly excused himself and walked away.

Returning to the taxi, the two hugged each other as they left the cemetery. It was their last goodbye to Michael–beloved brother and best friend.

Harper spent the rest of the day showing Laken her favorite places in Boston. They had lobster rolls to compare to the ones in San Francisco. Laken grudgingly admitted that the ones in Boston were much better than those in San Francisco. The two of them laughed at the mess they had made eating the buttery sandwiches. They visited the famous historical sites of the Boston Common, Bunker Hill, Old North Church, Old South Meeting House, and walked the grounds of Harvard. Harper enjoyed sharing her favorite site of Old North Church with Laken, and he shared that his favorite site was viewing the grounds of Harvard. He said that he felt closer to her after walking the same areas where she had. A dinner of clam chowder and rolls concluded the evening.

That night, their lovemaking was slow and gentle. It was as if they both needed to reaffirm their own mortality. For Laken, it was an unspoken declaration of his love for Harper. He couldn't say it out loud until he told her the full truth of himself and accepted him fully. It was still too soon in their relationship, and he wasn't quite ready to bring up such a sensitive topic after the emotional time they had just gone through.

Chapter 8

OVER the next three weeks, after returning from Boston, they developed a routine together. During the weekdays, Laken worked at the office, and Harper worked on her thesis at home, despite not being enrolled in a program. She had been too late to register for the semester at San Francisco State University.

One evening, Laken had arrived home to find Harper sitting on the floor of the office with photocopies, books, notes, and a notebook surrounding her. She had been muttering to herself while shuffling 3x5 cards and trying to organize chaos. He glanced over her shoulder and saw lists of "roles: alpha, beta, gamma, omega" and "powers: agility, balance, dexterity, durability, invulnerability, endurance, health, immunity, leap, reflexes, senses, speed, stamina, strength, healing, regeneration, immunity, instincts, tracking, stealth," as well as "aka: Homo Sapien Lupus, Lycan, Lycanthrope, Lycanthropy, Lupine, Wolfman/Wolfwoman, Wolf Therian, Garou." The stylistic script made it hard for Laken to read the writing without looking at it closely. Of the artworks, he recognized one from the 17th century. It went with the story of when someone found a lone werewolf scavenging for food. That was the story within the werewolf community. Within the human world, the werewolf was out to destroy property and find a human victim.

Harper was so engrossed in her research that she had never heard Laken enter nor glanced over her shoulder. He had to touch her shoulder to get her attention and ask her about the papers that she had laid out.

"What're you doing?" Laken asked Harper.

Looking up at him from the floor, Harper grinned at her husband. "Just trying to organize my notes and other research. I'm not sure if I'm succeeding or making more of a mess, though."

Laken leaned over and kissed the top of Harper's hair. He continued to have concerns about her research. Now would be as good a time as any for him to ask how far her research proved the existence of werewolves.

"You said that your Master's thesis was to prove the existence of werewolves. What has your research shown so far?" he asked.

Harper sighed. "That's a tough question to answer. I've found that there are a lot of stories and anecdotal proof of those stories. Such as this." She pointed to the artwork Laken had recognized. "This art illustrates a story that is in a manuscript. However, there is nothing to be found that is an actual event."

Nodding, Laken made sympathetic sounds while in his head he and Enzo both cheered.

"I've yet to find any concrete evidence of werewolf existence, but I haven't exhausted all resources, either. It'll be easier once I have access to the university archives again." She continued. "But since you're home, I'm going to be done for now."

Harper stood up and gathered the piles she had made, placing binder clips on them, then storing them in folders she kept on her desk. Seeing he wasn't needed, Laken kissed her head and said he'd see her at dinner after his shower.

It had become their habit that Laken would return from work to have dinner with Harper. Usually, she would have instructed the chef on what to prepare, though occasionally she would get caught up in her research. On those nights, dinner would be late or takeout. Later, after catching up on their day, they spent the night making love. On the weekends, they spent the time together doing everything from watching movies to visiting museums. Harper and Laken truly became a couple during these weeks.

Harper looked at the pregnancy test in her hand. Positive. Would Laken be happy? They had been married for barely six weeks and intimate for only five. Harper had really never been one to track her menstrual cycle. She had lost track of time since returning from Boston and just realized that she hadn't gotten her period since right before the last dinner with Michael. Since then, everything had happened so quickly, and the realization that she had missed her period had been the sign for her to take a test. Morning sickness and fatigue, typically expected in early pregnancy according to books and articles, were absent in her case. She looked at herself in the mirror as she placed her hand on her still-flat stomach and smiled. Harper had not really given a lot of thought to being a mother yet. She knew she wanted to have a family, but more in the future thing. Knowing she had a life growing inside of her now made her excited.

She tucked the pregnancy test into her purse and headed downstairs. She would need to find the right time to tell Laken.

Halfway down the stairs, the doorbell rang, so she went to answer it. Opening the door, she found a woman wearing a red mini dress and black stiletto heels with a black moto jacket on her arm, standing there with two suitcases. The smile on the woman's face disappeared, and she narrowed her kohl-lined eyes as she asked Harper, "Who the hell are you?"

Laken stepped beside Harper, taking her hand, and said, "She's my wife, Adria. I think you owe her an apology."

Adria gasped. "Your wife? I leave for a year, and you get married?"

"Who is this, Laken?" Harper asked, letting go of his hand and stepping back.

Adria smiled and brushed her long black hair over one shoulder, careful not to knock the design-er sunglasses off her head. "I'm his fiance." She stepped forward, attempting to wrap her arms around Laken and kiss him with her red-glazed lips.

Laken pulled himself away from her and said, "No, you are not."

Laken looked at Adria and said to her, "Get out of here. We were never engaged, and I told you that the last time I saw you. Harper is my mate." He then attempted to close the door in her face.

"Laken, I've nowhere to go. I just returned from abroad. Can I stay here for a couple of days while I find a new place to rent?" pouted Adria.

Gritting his teeth, Laken couldn't deny her request. As Alpha, the entire pack knew that if there was ever a need, he had guest rooms that werewolves could use. "Only for two days, Adria. That is it."

Harper looked from one to the other, then turned and ran up the stairs. Taking the stairs two at a time, Laken followed Harper. He found their bedroom door locked. He knocked on it and could hear her crying inside. "Harper, Adria is nothing to me. I promise. Please let me in so we can talk."

"Please go away, Laken," Harper replied through her sobs.

"Adria is just an acquaintance," Laken explained. "She is not my fiance, nor was she ever. Before she left overseas, she was constantly trying to be in places so we could be together. I resisted all her advances, and this was one reason her family sent her away."

Harper asked, "Then why would you give her a place to stay?"

"As she said, Adria just returned to town and needed a place to stay. I owed her family a favor, and she called it in."

Laying his head against the door, Laken pleaded with Harper to let him in once again.

"Harper, open the door. I've explained twice now that Adria is nothing to me. Let's continue this face to face."

Silence greeted him in response.

Laken told her, "I'll go for now, but we have to talk, my moonflower. I'm going to the office for a few hours while you calm down. There is something very important that I need to take care of. I'll see you later."

Harper came down for lunch and ran into Adria. She tried to head back upstairs, not wanting to talk to the woman, but Adria blocked Harper's way.

"So, how did you convince Laken to marry you?" asked Adria. "You're just a human."

Harper looked at her confused. "What are you talking about?"

Adria threw back her head and laughed. "You don't know, do you? Laken is a werewolf. We're all werewolves, you silly girl."

Werewolves? Adria had to be crazy, right? There is no such thing as werewolves. Except, isn't that exactly what she was trying to prove with her Master's thesis?

Adria continued, "I should be Laken's Luna, not you. How could you help the pack? You have no power, no gifts. I was going to marry him but left to go to Europe. I made a mistake leaving him, but now I'm back."

Harper knew enough from her research into werewolf lore to understand the terms *alpha*, *luna*, and *pack*. Maybe it was all true. It would also explain the mention of the Moon Goddess from Laken in the heat of their lovemaking that one night.

Adria crossed her arms and spat more derisive words at Harper. "I heard that Laken only married you as a deathbed promise to your brother. I can only imagine that he's going to keep it until he's tired of you. Or the next full moon. Then he can sacrifice you to the Moon Goddess for the ceremony."

"What?" Harper took a step back, stumbling against the staircase and grabbing hold of the railing to prevent falling.

"You heard me. Every nine years, we must sacrifice a human to let werewolves remain human and prevent them from becoming wolves permanently. Have you heard of the myth of Lycaon?" asked Adria.

Harper went pale. Of course, she had heard of it, as it was part of her thesis research. A scroll written by Plato from 400 BC told of the story between Zeus and the House of Lycaon. It spoke of a festival being held, including a banquet with human sacrifice to Zeus.

"Maybe you're to be the sacrifice at the full moon, which is in three days." Adria said with a wicked smile.

Harper turned and ran up the stairs with the sound of Adria's laughter trailing behind her. She went to the office that she and Laken shared. If there were proof that he was a werewolf, wouldn't she find it there?

In the office, Harper started by looking at the books on the bookshelves. She had only glanced at them before, but not really paid attention to them in depth. She doubted he would have left anything out in the open, but it was a place to start.

Finding nothing on the bookshelves, she moved to his desk. She bit her lip as she looked through the papers on top. There was a feeling of violating his privacy, but she needed to know the truth. If Adria was lying and she found no evidence, then all would be fine. However, if she found proof that showed Laken was a werewolf, she needed to protect herself and their child.

Their child. If Laken were a werewolf, would their child be half werewolf? A hybrid? Harper shook her head. She would have to figure that out later.

Harper opened the drawers one by one and sifted through the papers, books, and envelopes in them. In one, she dropped the stapler she had in her hand, and it thudded when it fell. It made a hollow sound, and she looked suspiciously at the drawer. She took all the items out of the drawer and noticed a small hole in the very back left corner. Using the point of the letter opener in the desk organizer, she lifted the false bottom. It revealed an ancient book, a sealing stamp, a wooden box, and a token that were equally old, as well as a scroll. There was also a bottle of ink, a fountain pen, and sealing wax.

Lifting the leather-bound book, Harper saw it lacked writing on the cover or spine, but metal latches secured it, and the pages were linen. She opened it carefully to see that it started with a list of werewolf roles in a pack. She slammed the book shut, not needing to read any more.

Harper put her hand on her heart, which was thumping out of control. Taking out her phone, she snaps photos of the items in the drawers. She would email her mentor professor and see if he thought these were genuine. If he said they were, then this was proof enough. It would show that Laken was a werewolf and werewolves were real.

It was much later than Laken expected when he arrived home. The San Francisco Area werewolf pack had annexed the Oakland-Berkeley pack that day, and the paperwork and subsequent celebration had lasted longer than he had thought. He had texted Harper that he would be home late, but she hadn't responded. Laken assumed it meant that she was still upset with him.

Opening the door to the bedroom, he could just make out Harper's shape under the covers on the bed. The lights were off, and it looked like she was already asleep.

Laken headed to the bathroom and then the dressing room to clean up and change. He then slid into bed and attempted to pull Harper close to him. She stiffened and said, "No."

Stopping, he said, "I wanted to talk before, but work held me up. I texted you. I'm sorry." Rolling over, he knew that sleep would be awhile in coming.

Chapter 9

HARPER feigned sleep when she heard Laken's alarm go off in the morning. She didn't want to face him. She knew she had to leave. If not for her sake, then definitely for her baby's.

Laken had lied to her about who he was. She didn't completely trust what Adria said, but she also didn't trust Laken. Not anymore. Right before bed, she had received an email from her mentor professor with confirmation that the items she had found were real. He had asked where she had found them and if he could borrow them to determine better authenticity. The items were from the 18th century and were definitely werewolf occult ceremony artifacts. Harper always found it interesting that academia considered werewolves "occult." This was confirmation to her that Laken must be a werewolf, like Adria said.

First, she needed to get money and find a place to live. How to do that without Laken finding her would be the tough part. She would go to the bank and pull out as much cash as she could. Then she would pay cash for anything she would need from here on out. It would be untraceable. She would use Harper Deveraugh on paper for any agreements or paperwork. She still had her Massachusetts license to back up that name if there was a need for verification.

Packing her overnight bag with just the basic items that she would need, she looked around the bedroom one more time. How could she go from being so happy to running away in less than a day?

She picked up the bag, her purse, and her phone. Harper would need to switch her phone right away, but needed information from it before tossing it. She knew Laken could trace her with it.

Harper walked down the stairs and out the front door. She didn't see Adria watching from just inside the sitting room with a smile on her face. Her plan had worked.

If only Laken had marked Harper when he had the chance, he wouldn't have had to turn to the police first and then the private investigators to find her. He hadn't wanted to push her when she didn't yet know he was a werewolf or understand werewolf mating rituals.

He would have been able to find her within days. Instead, it had been over eight weeks and there were still no leads where she had gone. Christmas and New Year had come and gone without news of her.

Laken had returned home from work that day only to find Adria and no Harper. Adria had said that Harper had just left. She had told him that now they could be together and she could be his Luna. He had railed at her and thrown her out.

No cars were missing from the garage, but Harper had taken her overnight bag and some clothes. His security camera had shown her getting into a cab outside the front gate. He had called the taxi company and found out that she had gone to the Bank of San Francisco.

The video surveillance at the bank had shown Harper withdrawing some of the money left to her by Michael. She couldn't withdraw all of it, but had taken the maximum amount. The cameras hadn't shown if someone had been there with her, making her take out the money. *Had she met someone at the bank? Or had she taken the money out on her own?* He didn't know if she had left him on her own or if someone had forced her to leave him.

Once she had left the bank, he couldn't trace her. No surveillance from the bank or any businesses nearby had caught her getting into a taxi or car. She had just disappeared.

Sitting in the study at home, Laken ran his hand down his face. He could feel the scruffiness of his beard. He had ceased to care about anything except finding Harper. Looking down, he took a drink from the glass in his hand. What did life matter without Harper in it?

After taking a single sip from the glass, Laken threw it against the wall. He needed to get out of here. The pack owned land outside the city where members could shift and run. He decided that was exactly what he should do. Laken grabbed the keys to one of his cars and set off on the 45-minute drive out of town. When he arrived at the secluded, fenced-in land that the pack owned, he scanned his card to open the gate. He drove up to and parked at the building that had changing rooms.

As he was the only one currently there, he gave up caution and stripped off his clothes, tossing them into the car. Laken shifted into Enzo's form and took off at a full run. If nothing else, this would wear him out and possibly let him sleep for the first time in weeks.

Laken stood at the bank of windows in his office on the top floor of Wolffang Enterprises. It had been seven months since Harper had walked out of his house and out of his life. His fist hit the wooden post dividing two of the windows, leaving a dent and rattling both the frame and windows. How can a woman just disappear? Especially a human? Did she not know how much she meant to him? If she had left on her own, did she realize how much she had hurt him? Apparently not, nor did she seem to care.

He came to work every day just to do something be-sides sit at home and drink. Everywhere he looked at home brought memories of Harper. Remember-ing how they had laughed at dinner, worked together in the office, and seeing the places they had made love. Tatum was running the place. Laken now served only as a figurehead. He knew that everyone around him was worried about him. He had lost weight and did nothing but watch his phone to see if a call came in from the agency.

Even Alana and Paxton, the fraternal twins who represented the Omegas on the council, came to the office one day. They had come on behalf of the council to check on him. He hadn't just been abandoning his duties at Wolffang Enterprises but also as the Alpha of the San Francisco Area werewolf pack. However, seeing him as he was, they reported to the council to implement the executive plan for trusteeship. Laken didn't disagree or fight the decision when he heard about it.

Laken laid his forehead against the cold glass of the window. *Where are you, Harper? Please be safe.* He thought for the millionth time.

There was a knock on the door. Tatum stuck his head inside and said, "Laken, Adria is here again."

Growling, Laken turned and glared at his Beta. "Why can't that bitch take a hint?"

Adria had been coming to the office once a week since he had kicked her out of his house. She kept insisting on trying to see him, telling staff she was his fiance even though everyone at the office knew he was married. The woman was insane, obsessed with him.

The phone in Laken's pocket vibrated. He pulled it out and immediately answered it. It was the private investigation agency. "We've found her." His eyes closed in prayer, *Thank the Moon Goddess.*

Laken looked at Tatum. "Tell Adria she can go to hell. I need my car ready NOW. They've found Harper."

Laken watched his wife through the glass of the insurance agency window. All this time, she had still been on the other side of the San Francisco Bay in Oakland, still in his pack territory. The private investigator had explained that he had found Harper through the tax documents that had come through with her maiden name on them. She had filed her taxes on the last filing date by paper, which is why it had taken so long for them to be found. These had revealed where she had been living and working.

Now he sat in his car parked on the other side of the street, wondering how to confront her, but also relieved to see Harper and know that she was safe. Inside, Enzo was going crazy, insisting that he barge into the building and mark her immediately.

Tatum looked at him and asked, "What do you want to do now, Alpha?"

Laken turned to his Beta. "I honestly don't know. I still don't know why she left. She doesn't seem forced to leave, so if she doesn't want to be with me, I won't force her. But we need to talk, just not at her work."

Laken looked back towards the insurance agency. At that moment, Harper stood up and walked around the desk, where she had been sitting to help a customer with some brochures. He inhaled in shock, as it was now clear that she was heavily pregnant. Without further thought, Laken ripped the car door open and ran across the road, heedless of the cars honking at him. If people had looked closer, they would have seen a glimmer of red in his eyes, as his wolf was dangerously close to the surface.

Harper turned to look at what was causing the ruckus outside the office. That's when she saw Laken pull open the door to the insurance agency and rush towards her.

How had he found her? She had done so much to keep under the radar and prevent being found. After she had fled the house and withdrew money from the bank, she had rented out a room in one of those pay by the week motels for a month, used the bus for transportation with a prepaid transit card, and went to a women's shelter for a prenatal check. She had been careful to pay in cash for everything.

Harper found a landlord who was willing not to run a credit check if she paid up front for six months, as well as the security deposit in cash. She had also been lucky when one of the volunteer doctors at the women's shelter had noticed her changing her address for the prenatal clinic and offered to see her at her office since it was near the new apartment. The shelter found her explanation regarding her estranged husband and lack of insurance credible; therefore, she paid cash.

Luckily, she had also found this job within walking distance of the apartment. She had asked to be paid in cash, but that hadn't been possible. There was a check-cashing place nearby, though, so she used that instead of a bank. They had only required her to show her ID for transactions. Turns out all her cautiousness had been for nothing.

"No!" she yelled and backed away from him, trying to put her desk between them, cradling her belly.

The sight startled the customer she had been helping, and he backed out the door. Harper glanced quickly at the door to see the customer running down the sidewalk.

"Harper! Is this why you left me?" Laken asked, grabbing her arm in his hand. Enzo growled in his head, demanding that he mark her now, seeing that his pup was in her. He had to tamp down the thought and his wolf. Now was not the time to lose control.

Harper ignored his question and asked one of her own. "How did you find me, Laken? Why did you look for me?" She tried to pull her arm away.

"Why?! What do you mean, why? You're my wife! I've been looking for you since the day you disappeared. I thought something horrible had happened to you!" Laken practically yelled.

Sally Fallenhyde, Harper's boss, came out of her office to see what all the yelling was about. She stopped upon seeing her Alpha standing next to her employee and holding her arm.

"May I ask what is going on?" she asked. She had to be polite to Alpha Laken, but played it safe, knowing that Harper was a human and couldn't know that she and Laken were werewolves.

"This is my WIFE," Laken said through gritted teeth. "And I'm leaving with her now."

Harper faced him down. "No, I am not going anywhere with you!"

Sally gasped, "Harper, you told me your husband was dead! But he's really Al..., I mean, here now."

"He may as well be dead for the lies and deception between us!" she hissed at Laken, finally pulling her arm away.

Laken looked at her in surprise. "Lies? I'm not the one who disappeared saying nothing seven months ago!"

"Sir, I'm so sorry, I didn't know," started Sally to Laken.

He cut her off with a swipe of his hand. "Enough. Let's go," he said, turning to Harper.

She crossed her hands over her chest. "I am not going anywhere." Then suddenly Harper bent over her belly, clutched her head, and groaned. "Nooooo."

"What is it?" Laken rushed to her side just as Harper fell. He scooped her into his arms, having to adjust his hold because of the difference in her weight from the pregnancy.

Sally broke in, "She's been dealing with high blood pressure. Her doctor wanted her to cut her hours at work, but Harper refused. I was going to make her after this week since she's now 33 weeks along."

33 weeks? That means she was eight months pregnant! He thought. *She knew she was pregnant when she left me. Why did she leave when she was pregnant? I thought we were happy and in love?*

Laken demanded, "Where's the closest hospital?"

"The Alta Bates Summit Medical Center is about 2 miles away. I'll grab you her purse," said Sally.

Pushing the door open, Laken looked towards the car where Tatum waited. He motioned with his head to bring the car to the curb. Tatum immediately crossed the three lanes of one-way traffic to do so. Sally opened the back-seat car door for him, and he climbed inside, setting Harper on the seat with her head on his lap. She handed him her purse.

"I'll send Tatum back to finish things with you. Harper no longer works for you," he said curtly.

Sally bowed her head. "Of course, Alpha."

"Go quickly to the Alta Bates hospital," demanded Laken. He brushed the hair back from Harper's face. It had grown longer during their time apart. "I just found you, my moonflower. I can't lose you now."

Harper moaned from where she lay and whispered. "Please, Laken, don't hurt the baby."

Laken frowned. *What did she mean?*

Chapter 10

TATUM pulled the car to the front of the ER doors of the medical center. He got out and opened the door for Laken, who was already lifting Harper into his arms. Ignoring the guard who was coming to ask what the need was, Laken walked past him and into the vestibule.

"My wife is eight months pregnant and passed out," he said to the guard, who immediately recognized the authority in his voice and opened the doors. Turning to Tatum, he continued, "Go back to the insurance agency. Get Harper's information from Sally. Move all her items back to my house and close out anything with Sally regarding Harper's employment."

Tatum replied, "Yes, sir," and turned back to the car to leave and do as his Alpha commanded.

The guard told Laken to follow him and took him right to triage. The nurse took one look and led them through the triage to a room.

In the room, a nurse took Harper's blood pressure, announcing it was 138 over 102. The high blood pressure reading prompted others in the room to rush, and they pushed Laken aside. He felt fear squeeze his heart. Another nurse pulled him out of the room.

"Sir, Ms. Deveraugh's blood pressure is quite high, and we need to give her fluids. The doctor will be in shortly, but a review of her notes shows that when she was last seen by the obstetrician, he recommended she quit her job. Do you know whether she has done this?" the nurse asked.

Laken hissed at the woman, "Her name is Mrs. Howlkind. She is my WIFE!"

The nurse took a step back because of the animosity in his voice. "I'm sorry, sir, I'm going off with her registration information. Our system shows her registration as Harper Deveraugh."

"Change it then!" he demanded. "And no, she didn't stop working. But she has as of today."

"Yes, sir. If you can wait out here, I'll have the doctor talk to you soon," the nurse assured him.

Laken paced in the hallway, stopping every time someone went in or came out of the room. He also couldn't stop thinking about the plea that Harper had whispered to him. *Why would she think he would hurt their child?*

He pulled out his phone to see a text from Tatum, who was at the apartment that Harper had been renting. He wanted to know what to do with the furniture in it, specifically the nursery that she had set up in the second bedroom. This caused Laken to pause. He had yet to think much about the pup.

Laken texted Tatum to move the nursery items to the guest room closest to the main suite in the house. He would hire an interior designer to change the guest room into a nursery. Next, he told Tatum to leave the other furniture for now and just bring Harper's clothing, toiletries, and anything else he thought necessary to the house. He also asked Tatum to pay that month's rent prior to leaving.

As he finished the last text, a man came out of the room and stopped in front of him. "I understand you're Ms. Deveraugh's husband?" asked the doctor.

"I keep telling your staff, Harper is Mrs. Howlkind!" growled Laken.

The doctor clarified, "Sir, I apologize, but we can only go off of what our registration records say."

Laken frowned at the man, but realized he couldn't argue anymore. "Fine. What is the news about my wife?"

"Harper is doing better with the fluids we've given her. Her blood pressure is down but still higher than I would like. She has an appointment with her OB next Monday, so I don't think she needs to be seen right away. I would like her to stop working and keep off her feet as much as possible. She should also avoid any undue stress. Her due date is six and a half weeks away. If she doesn't follow these instructions, she may end up on full bed rest or have early labor. We also did an exam and determined that the baby is fine. The heartbeat is strong, with no signs of distress."

Laken felt such relief that he fell back against the wall. Both Harper and the baby were okay.

"When can I take Harper home?" he asked.

The doctor replied, "I want her to finish this bag of fluids, and then the nurse can remove the IV. So maybe 30-45 minutes. You can go in and sit with her now if you'd like." Shaking Laken's hand, the doctor left.

Laken looked toward the room where Harper was. He wanted to go in badly, but would she want him there? Looking through the window, he saw she was lying on her side, curled in a ball around her belly. He took a breath and opened the door. It closed softly behind him.

"Harper?" he asked.

"Please go away, Laken," was her response. "I've nothing to say to you." She refused to look at him.

He walked over to the side of the bed and squatted next to it. He tried to take her hand, but she pulled it away. Laken looked down at the floor. "We'll need to talk, but this isn't the place. The doctor told me you would be discharged soon. Then I'm taking you back home."

At that, Harper looked at him in shock. "No! I don't want..." she started.

"You can't work anymore, have to be off your feet, and need to be taken care of or you will go into early labor. How can you do that living alone? I've already had Tatum move yours and the baby's things to the house. I'll have the guest room redecorated into a nursery." explained Laken.

"How dare you!" Harper exclaimed. "I can hire someone instead of living with you!" She tried to turn away, but her bulk wouldn't allow her to, so she turned her head instead and closed her eyes.

Laken took hold of her chin and pulled her face back to look at him. "This is my child too, or did you forget? I want a say in this. You have denied me eight months of this pregnancy!"

Opening her eyes, Harper saw something on his face and gave in. "For the baby, I'll stay in the guest room. But we need to talk and figure things out. Later. Right now, I want to take a nap. Please go away." She closed her eyes again, pretending to rest.

After discharge, Tatum picked them up from the hospital and drove them to the house. Harper sat in the backseat, alternately furious about being forced back to the house that she fled and tired of trying so hard to hide from Laken. She looked out the window. How would she deal with seeing Adria and Laken together day after day?

The car pulled up at the house. Before Laken could get out of the car and open the door for Harper, she did it herself. He growled and lifted her into his arms before she could take a step.

"What are you doing?" she demanded.

He replied to her question, "The doctor said you are to stay off your feet. What part of that did you not understand?"

Harper slapped at his shoulders. "So what are you going to do, carry me everywhere? He didn't literally mean that I can't walk, so put me down."

Laken ignored her and carried her into the house and up the stairs to the room that used to be their bedroom. He sat her down on the edge of the bed.

"Why are we here? You said I would be in the guest room," demanded Harper.

"No, you said you would be in the guest room. I said that would be the nursery. Why wouldn't my wife be in our bedroom?" countered Laken. He knelt down to take off her shoes, but she toed them off herself.

Harper crossed her arms in front of her and looked down at him. "Won't Adria be upset that you plan to share your room with me instead of her?"

"Adria? What does she have to do with anything?" He asked, perplexed. "She's not even here and hasn't been for months. I kicked her out the day you disappeared. I told you then that there was nothing between Adria and me. Is that why you left?" Laken took Harper by the arms.

"No, that is not why I left!" she exclaimed, pulling away and scooting back by the headboard of the bed. "Now, I'm tired. Could you please leave me alone?"

Laken looked at her, knowing that she was avoiding talking about things. He also realized that pushing her wouldn't do any good. They needed to reconcile, not just for the baby, but for their own relationship with each other. He still loved her, but needed to find out what had made her leave. For that conversation to happen, she needed to be calm, and she wasn't right now.

"I'll have Mrs. Redmoon bring up your dinner on a tray. I have to do some work at the office. Use the voice commands or the tablet to contact me or the other staff if you need anything," said Laken.

Running his fingers through his hair, Laken stifled a yawn. He had wasted as much time as possible in the office to avoid going back to the bedroom. He didn't want to start another fight with Harper. The doctor had said that she needed to avoid stress.

Laken entered the bedroom and heard the soft, even sound that showed Harper was asleep. He breathed a sigh of relief and got himself ready for bed. Sliding between the covers, he moved as close as he dared to his mate, falling into the deepest sleep he had been in for months.

Harper slowly came awake, feeling the baby kicking and desperately needing to use the bathroom. Both were becoming more frequent occurrences of late. She opened her eyes and remembered that she was in Laken's house and bed.

It was also then that she realized the baby was kicking because of the weight that was resting over the mound of her belly. Laken's arm. He must have come to bed after she had fallen asleep.

She slid out from under his arm and walked to the bathroom, for the first time wishing it had a door. Previously, she had always admired the open-concept design. Harper took care of her needs, then walked back to find that Laken had awoken.

She felt exposed standing in the bathroom doorway with him watching her. While she was away, she had thought he had been cheating on her with Adria. Thoughts of them together had fueled her animosity and hatred and the idea that he had used her. To find out that Laken had kicked Adria out the day Harper had left changed what she thought of him. Had she been wrong about everything else?

Harper didn't realize that with the light coming in from the bathroom windows, it highlighted her from behind. To Laken, the light silhouetted her, making her look like the painting of the Madonna and Child.

"Are you okay?" Laken asked. "I'll leave so you can return to bed." He left the bed and headed to the dressing room.

Harper returned to the bed and between the covers. Propping herself against the headboard so she was sitting up, she replied, "I'm fine. Using the bathroom is a frequent thing at this stage of pregnancy."

Laken paused while buttoning up his shirt and raised an eyebrow. Really? Interesting. He had a lot to learn about pregnancy.

Popping his head around the corner of the dressing room, Laken looked at her. "You're to stay here and rest like the doctor said. Ask the staff for anything you need. I'll be heading into the office today, but I'm also going to call and schedule an interior designer to come and talk to you about the nursery. I'll set it up for after lunch." He returned to the dressing room to finish getting ready.

Harper glared at Laken. "What? I agreed to stay in the guest room and said that we needed to talk. You can't dictate my life!"

"I'm making sure you follow the instructions from the doctor. You're supposed to be off your feet, remember? How can you do that by yourself? I need you here where I can monitor you," he demanded.

Laken continued, "And as I mentioned, this is my baby, too. He or she needs the nursery set up, and I thought you would like to help decorate it. I also plan to go to the doctor's appointment on Monday. From here on out, I plan to be part of everything."

Going to the bedroom door, Laken stormed out and headed down the stairs. So much for not arguing. He couldn't seem to say the right things to Harper anymore. Halfway down, he thought about how he would have to text Harper about the time when the interior designer would be over, then swore out loud.

He didn't have her number. He turned and headed back up the stairs. Harper looked at Laken when he unexpectedly returned to the room.

"I need your number," Laken demanded.

Harper picked up her cell phone from the bedside stand and pressed a few buttons. In his hand, Laken's phone buzzed with a text message.

His brow raised in surprise. "Did you have my number already on your phone?"

Refusing to answer, Harper turned and looked out the window.

"I'll text you when the interior designer will be over," Laken said to her as he turned to leave again.

Chapter 11

H EARING a knock on the bedroom door, Harper said, "Come in."

Mrs. Redmoon, the housekeeper, entered with a tray. She had always been kind to Harper.

"It's so nice to have you back, Mrs. Howlkind. Mr. Laken asked me to bring you breakfast. Please let me know if there is anything else that you'll need," said Mrs. Redmoon.

"Thank you, Mrs. Redmoon. Laken said that Tatum brought over things from my apartment. Do you know where my laptop is?" she asked.

Mrs. Redmoon replied, "Yes, ma'am. I put it on your old desk in the office. I'll get it for you."

She immediately fetched the laptop and returned with it to Harper. Harper was glad to have it as something to keep herself occupied. She may have to look for other ways to entertain herself for the next six weeks. Without going to work, she could imagine that she would become bored fairly easily.

Upon finishing breakfast, Harper received the text from Laken that the interior designer would arrive at 1pm. At least she had that to look forward to today.

Later that afternoon, Harper met with the interior designer in the bedroom, in the sitting area. The designer reviewed the furniture and items moved from Harper's apartment. He quickly recognized that she preferred a contemporary style, which helped him with some preliminary designs. Harper explained she wanted to have the bassinet in the bedroom with her for the beginning and that it was a convertible bassinet/crib/toddler bed. The designer loved it and knew exactly how he would incorporate it into his design.

Harper found an excitement in that her previous baby purchases fit in the guest room, even though Laken compelled her to stay at his house. The interior designer understood how she wanted to be connected with her baby initially and have a functional but natural space for the baby. The designer would come by the following Tuesday with his last designs, then be able to begin the redecorating in another week.

The interior designer called Laken with an update after meeting with Harper. Laken told him that there was no budget limit, and that Harper was in control of everything. After confirming the contract that was emailed over, he settled in for a long afternoon and late night. He figured it was better to work as much as possible to avoid any more fights with Harper. This vied with his desire to be near her, but he felt it was better to stay away for the next few days until she settled in and calmed down.

He called in Tatum and asked him to order him some dinner to be delivered later. He returned to his computer and the paperwork on his desk, and tackled the work that had accumulated during his self-absorption while Harper was missing.

Monday dawned to another day of Harper feeling like a prisoner. She had spent the weekend in bed looking through Amazon to buy things for her to do. She had purchased an ebook reader, puzzle board, a couple puzzles, colored pencils, and an adult coloring book. They would arrive the next day. She was looking forward to having some extra activities to do.

Today, though, was the latest prenatal checkup, and Laken insisted he was coming along. Harper still didn't know how she felt about it. Her appointment was   first thing that morning, and she had already dressed and eaten breakfast.

Laken opened the bedroom door. "Are you ready?" he asked.

Harper nodded, turning and climbing off the bed. Laken hurried around the bed and picked her up. "Put me down, Laken!" said Harper.

Laken explained, "You can't walk down all the stairs. I'll put you down when I get to the car." He carried her down the staircase and to the car, where he set her down. Opening the car door, Laken helped her slide into the passenger seat before walking around to the driver's side.

The ride to the obstetrician's office was quiet. It was in Oakland, which would take about twenty-five minutes to get to from the house. Since Harper was close to term, it was better to continue with the same doctor than to switch.

Arriving at the office, Laken dropped Harper off at the front door, then parked the car. He asked Harper to wait for him in the lobby. Upon entering, he found Harper was waiting. He checked her in for the appointment and then asked for a wheelchair for her. Harper didn't argue with him this time.

Laken pushed the wheelchair to the waiting room and then to their assigned checkup room, appearing to everyone as a doting father and husband. He then helped Harper up onto the exam table. The nurse who accompanied them took her vitals, happy with the normal blood pressure.

Once the nurse was done, the doctor was immediately behind her. She reviewed the notes and did her own checks. When she pushed up Harper's top to measure her belly, Laken asked what was going on. The doctor explained that she was measuring the belly to compare against the number of weeks of the pregnancy.

Laken realized how much he needed to learn and pulled out his phone. While the doctor continued with her regular diagnostics, he opened his e-reader app and looked up "best new father pregnancy guide." He found the best-rated book, purchased it, and downloaded it. He planned to read it later that day when he spent time at the office.

He realized the doctor was speaking and paid attention to what was being said. Because of the issues with Harper's high blood pressure and passing out the week before, the doctor wanted her to have an ultrasound to check the amniotic fluid levels. She said that the tech would be right in to do it. After the test, they would be ready to leave, but the doctor wanted to see Harper weekly for checkups until her delivery.

When the tech came in, she explained what would happen and asked if they wanted to find out the sex since at the last ultrasound; the baby hadn't been cooperative. Harper looked at Laken questioningly.

"Can we find out what the baby is?" he asked.

The tech replied, "Most likely, yes. At the 20-week ultrasound, the baby was still quite small and not cooperative with its positioning to view its gender."

Harper told the tech, "Then yes, we'd like to find out."

"I'll do all the amniotic fluid measurements first, which will take me about fifteen minutes, then I can do that. I'll let you know when I'm done with the first part," said the tech.

The tech raised Harper's shirt, tucked in a couple of towels to protect her clothing, then put on the ultrasound gel. Harper held the top towel in place while the tech ran the ultrasound wand around her stomach to take the measurements. Laken watched in fascination at the images on the screen, trying to figure out what he was seeing.

Soon the tech announced she was done with the measurements and would do the imaging instead. She said that she would also print off pictures of the baby. She turned the screen to face them, so it was easier for Harper to see.

The screen showed a black-and-white image of a fetus. Laken became overwhelmed with emotion and unconsciously reached out to hold Harper's hand.

As the tech switched between different views, they could see their baby, its face, its foot, even sucking its thumb. The tech also changed from 2D to 3D views and printed out photos as she went along. At last she announced, "Congratulations, it's a boy!"

"My son?" asked Laken. "I have a son?"

"Yes, sir," said the tech.

Harper turned to look at him with tears in her eyes. It was the first time the two of them had truly been cordial since Laken had found her. "We have a baby boy."

Laken picked up Harper's hand and kissed her knuckles as he smiled at her. "Thank you, my moon-flower." It was the first time he had used his nickname for her since she had been back.

This new rapport continued through the next day. The interior designer came to meet with Harper to review the last design for the nursery. Harper fell in love with it on sight. It was exactly what she wanted. The designer had captured all of her ideas and wishes.

The designer explained he would start shopping for everything immediately and text her pictures of the items he found. His team would start on the nursery itself the next week. He also told her he would send the final numbers to Laken for review.

After the interior designer meeting, Harper laid down for a rest. She found she was getting more tired in the afternoons and would take a nap. After her nap, she awoke to find a text from Laken saying that he was working late again.

This was the third day he was working late. He had never worked late before she had left, and she wondered if he was avoiding her or if there was another reason he hadn't been coming home. Before she had left, she had thought she was falling in love with Laken. Now she was insecure about their entire relationship.

The two of them still hadn't really talked. She also hadn't asked him about being a werewolf, but in some ways, she didn't want to know either. Harper rolled over in the bed and looked out the window. Over the course of her time away, she had done more research about werewolves in the present. Previously, she had focused her research on werewolves in the past. Now she knew that many conspiracy theories out there said that werewolf packs existed. Though people believed they inhabited remote wild areas. Here they were in the middle of one of the most populated cities on the west coast. Was there really a werewolf pack in San Francisco?

Laken looked over the work on his desk. He was tired of hiding in his office. It was already late, but not as late as he had been staying the other two nights. He decided he would just pack up now.

Laken opened and closed the   bedroom door quietly before turning around. He wasn't expecting the scene he found.

Harper lay on the bed, eyes closed, arm above her head, nightgown rucked around her waist. With a bent knee, she rubbed the swollen bud between her legs and moaned softly.

He peeled off his tie, jacket, and shirt on his way to the bed. Laken took off his shoes and dropped his belt as well. As he crawled onto the mattress, Harper suddenly realized his presence from the shift she felt. She gasped and opened her eyes as Laken's hands pushed apart her thighs. His mouth replaced her hand as he sank between her legs.

Harper could only moan and close her eyes again as feelings overtook her. Her hands grasped handfuls of the sheets under her. Her hips raised slightly to meet Laken's mouth as his lips and teeth teased her sensitive area. She could feel the spasms start in her core and then wash over her.

Laken raised his head and wiped off his mouth with his hand, smiling. He looked up at his wife, who was in a post-orgasmic stupor. He recalled a chapter in the pregnancy book where it said that women in the late stage of pregnancy often had high libido and that sex was safe.

Harper was slow to recover from her climax. Her breathing slowed down, and she realized Laken was still between her legs, looking up at her. Mortification washed over her alternately because of what he had seen her do and what he had done to her.

She watched as Laken slid up the bed to lie next to her with his head in his hand. His face was unreadable, and she turned her eyes away rather than continue to look at him. She self-consciously smoothed her nightgown over her belly and legs back into place. Harper knew she was ungainly at this stage of the pregnancy, and her chest was the only thing appealing since it was a full cup size larger.

Laken reached out to brush Harper's hair from her face. Enzo ran circles in his head with the long-awaited contact with his mate. It had been so long since the two of them had touched without animosity between them. He ran his fingers down the side of her face, her neck, and then her arm. Leaning forward, he pressed a kiss to her cheek and said, "I'll be back."

Leaving the bed, Laken entered the bathroom and took a quick cold shower, then put on pajama bottoms. He returned to bed and pulled Harper to spoon with him. She didn't protest but settled in. Laken slid his arm around her swollen waist and rested it over where his child lay. The two fell asleep this way.

Chapter 12

THE following day, Harper awoke alone. When Mrs. Redmoon came in with her breakfast tray, Harper found out that Laken had left for a five-day trip unexpectedly. The disappointment that she felt because he hadn't told her was sudden and surprising. Mrs. Redmoon said that Laken promised he would be back in time for the doctor's appointment on Monday.

Adria had been watching Alpha Laken's house for a couple of days before she saw him leave early this day. She had heard the news that he had found his wife after months of searching. That little bitch had only moved across the bay and not run away like Adria had hoped. Not only had Laken brought her back, but she was pregnant with his pup now, too.

Despite trying to see him every day while Harper had been missing, Laken had refused to even see her. Adria had been in love with him for years and, as a Gamma, was more his equal than a mere human. She had been furious when her family had sent her away for her attempts to snare Laken almost two years ago. Why was this pathetic, weak human Alpha Laken's mate and not her? The only way to get rid of Harper now was to kill her. It would also break the mate bond, which would allow Adria to take over as Laken's new mate.

When Laken had left early, Adria had asked others in the pack for details without bringing too much attention to herself. She had found out that he had left for a sudden Alpha alliance meeting that should last for several days. This would give her time to put a plan in place and implement it before he came back. It was time to get rid of Harper.

The next five days seemed to drag by. Even though she had rarely seen Laken, not seeing him at all made Harper miss him more. She struggled with restlessness despite the new items she had bought to keep herself busy.

Harper questioned why she didn't feel anger towards him anymore. During her time at home, Laken did nothing to hurt herself or the baby. Instead, he has done everything to take care of them. Did he love them? And the better question: did she love him? When he returned, she vowed that the two of them would talk. They had to clear things up before the baby was born.

Harper awoke on Sunday hoping for the day to go by fast and Monday to come so Laken would come home. She waited until Mrs. Redmoon brought her breakfast, then took a shower. Sighing, she realized today would drag by unless she did something productive. Deciding, since it was such a nice day, that she would like to sit out on the balcony, Harper asked Mrs. Redmoon to help her move out here. Once settled, she worked on one of her puzzles. It engaged her until lunchtime. After lunch, the warm sun lulled her to sleep.

She awoke a few hours later when a shadow fell over her. Having opened her eyes, she saw a face she had never expected to see again. "What are you doing here?" Harper exclaimed just before someone pressed a cloth over her mouth and nose and she felt a prick to her neck.

Harper awoke again to find herself in some woods with tape over her mouth, rope tying her hands and feet. She was lying on her side on the ground while Adria stood over her holding a knife, which she was using to clean under her nails. Too distracted by the crazy woman looming over her, Harper missed the fact that all around her were the infamous California sequoia trees. She did notice that it was close to sunset. How long had she been unconscious?

"So, you're awake. I've been waiting for hours. That sedative worked a little too well on you," Adria said in a bored tone. "You didn't stay away like you were supposed to the first time, so I figure I have to get rid of you completely this time. Then Alpha Laken will be mine."

Her bonds prevented Harper from doing anything but listen in amazement to the insane woman, despite the dizziness from the drug injection. Adria meant to kill her and her baby. How could she get away? She had to save herself and her child.

Adria continued, "Well, I'm off to meet my mate. Enjoy your last hours under the stars." She cackled as she turned and walked away.

Harper's eyes widened; she was really being left out in the woods to die. This only happened in terrible movies and novels, not real life, right?

Think, Harper, think. How did the people get out of these situations? She thought to herself. *I need to get these ropes off first.*

Reaching as far as she could behind her with her fingers, she felt around to see what was on the ground. Harper found a rock that seemed to have a sharp edge and started rubbing it on the ropes, hoping that she could at least fray them. If she could, then she could twist or pull it enough to break it. It must have taken over ten minutes of wearing at the rope before the rock dulled and she had to find another. She scooted around the ground, found another and then repeated the process. Eventually, after finding a third rock, Harper could pull the rope apart and free her hands, and then untie her feet. She cut herself in several places during this process, but the cuts were shallow. Twisting and turning to cut the rope chafed her wrists. Neither the cuts nor the

chafing overly concerned her. It was more important that she was free.

Once she had the ropes off her wrists, Harper struggled to sit up and untie the ones off her ankles,
then tore the tape from her mouth. She had to take
several deep breaths after doing that because of the
skin that was removed with the adhesive. Looking
around, Harper tried to get her bearings. She had a
basic knowledge of how to tell where she was based
on the positions of the moon and the North Star.
She had been a Girl Scout when she was younger
and remembered that much from one of her badge
requirements. Since the moon was just rising in the
western sky and the North Star was right overhead,
she had to be northwest of San Francisco. Harper
headed southeast, hoping she would come across
a road, a house, or some other sign of humanity.

Laken felt exhausted after the sudden meeting of
the West Coast Alphas. It had been a long four
days of discussion and negotiations. Sitting around
a table trying to convince ten men and women, who
were all leaders of their own packs, to agree on
terms was a Herculean task. His large pack, reputa-

tion for fairness, and the respect of the other Alphas led to Laken's election as the group's facilitator. Some days, the Alphas had to take breaks to shift and literally run off steam. This added time to the process and frustrated Laken, as he just wanted to finish and go home to Harper.

On Sunday, Laken arrived home late. He rubbed the back of his neck as he trudged up the stairs, being extremely quiet so as not to wake Harper or Mrs. Redmoon, who had been staying there while he was gone. All he wanted at this time was to see and hold Harper. He had missed her more than he had thought he would.

He took his clothes off, letting them fall to the floor next to the bed, and climbed in wearing only his undershirt and briefs. After he pulled the sheet over himself, he reached out for Harper. Laken slid his hand across the bed several times, not finding her body or any warmth on the sheets. He sat up and turned on the light. His eyes widened in alarm when he didn't see her in the bed. He couldn't believe he had been so exhausted that he hadn't realized he didn't smell her scent before realizing she wasn't in the room at all.

Clambering out of   bed, Laken ran downstairs looking for Mrs. Redmoon. He found her sobbing in the kitchen. "Where is my wife?" he demanded.

Mrs. Redmoon looked up, startled to see him standing there as she hadn't heard him arrive home or enter the kitchen. "Alpha, I don't know where Mrs. Howlkind is. I took her lunch, and when I went to bring down the tray, she was asleep on the balcony. Figuring she could ring when she was awake, I left her alone and started on dinner and the cleaning. I lost track of time, realizing a few hours later that she hadn't asked for a snack. When I went back up, she was gone! I tried to call you, but it went to voicemail. When I couldn't reach you, I immediately contacted Beta Tatum, who came and reviewed the surveillance. Surveillance footage revealed two hooded figures ascending the stairs, then descending, one carrying an unconscious Mrs. Howlkind."

Looking at the housekeeper in surprise when she said she couldn't reach him by phone, Laken immediately went to look for it. He found his cell phone in his briefcase, still in silent mode. Upon picking it up, he noticed the missed calls and voicemails from Mrs. Redmoon and Beta Tatum. For the Alpha meeting, he had put it on silent ringer, but he had forgotten to change it before leaving for home. He had been so tired when he had gotten home he had also forgotten to take his phone out of his briefcase.

Laken growled, "How dare someone come into my home and take my mate! Where is Beta Tatum now?" He demanded of the housekeeper, who was sobbing again.

"Beta Tatum found the license plate of the car that took Luna. He went to Wolffang Enterprises to use the resources there to track it." explained Mrs. Red-moon.

Laken turned and left to go join his beta, making a call to Tatum at the same time to find out the status of the search for Harper. Tatum informed Laken that he, as well as the head Gammas, Raegan and Colt, and some of the other pack warriors, were on their way towards the pack's running grounds. The car that had taken Harper was last seen getting off the freeway at that exit. The only place off the exit was the running grounds, and its existence solely belonged to the members of the pack.

Informing Tatum that he would join him as soon as he could, Laken stepped on the gas and headed to join the others. Whoever had done this had better hope nothing happened to Harper or his child, oth-erwise there would be hell to pay.

After walking for several miles and needing to stop for breaks along the way, Harper came across a parking lot and small building. She found the building locked and, using a large rock from the edge of the parking lot, she bashed the locked door handle off. It took her five minutes to do this, and she had to stop halfway through to rip off part of her shirt and wrap it around her hands. Harper swore she would find out who owned the building and pay them back for the busted handle.

The building had bathrooms as well as what looked like changing rooms. It was an odd building to find in the middle of a wooded area, but at least it was a shelter from the night air. She also found some snacks and water inside that she took as a godsend since she hadn't eaten since breakfast. Harper sat in a chair and put her feet up on another. All the walking had caused her ankles to swell, and she knew it wasn't good in her condition.

Her biggest concern now was figuring out how to get ahold of Mrs. Redmoon or Laken and let them know where she was. Harper knew someone had discovered her disappearance. It had been several hours as far as she could tell since it was now fully dark outside. Mrs. Redmoon would have called Laken to tell him, and someone should look for her. She doubted anyone would know where to look for her.

Harper fell asleep in the chair, wondering about her next steps, too exhausted to stay awake. Little did she know that Laken and his warriors were heading her way.

Meeting the wolf pack members at the gate to the running grounds, Laken asked about the retrieval of the gate records. Raegan told him that the only card scanned that day was Adria's. A picture of the scan showed her in the driver's seat and an unknown male in the passenger seat. If Harper had been in the car, nobody saw her.

Laken slammed a fist into a nearby tree, scraping up his knuckles and causing them to bleed. Adria again. He had apparently not been harsh enough with that she-wolf the first time she interfered with him and his mate. Once Harper was home safe, he would deal with her and the accomplice she had hired.

Driving through the gate, the three cars parked at the changing building. Laken wanted to view the surveillance cameras that recorded the parking lot. He hoped to see which direction the car went into the woods. Walking into the building, he was shocked to find Harper asleep on the chair.

Laken rushed to Harper and checked her for injuries. He was running his hands down her arms when she woke up and started hitting him. "Harper, stop, it's me, Laken!" he said to her.

"Laken?" she asked. "Is it really you? How did you find me?"

He explained, "Tatum gets the credit for that. He's the one who tracked the car here. Some other friends of mine helped with rescuing you as well. They are all outside. Are you and the baby okay? Do you have any injuries?"

"Yes," she replied, "We both are. I have some cuts and rope burns on my wrists, but they aren't that bad. Right now, all I want is to go home. Please take me there."

Chapter 13

LAKEN carried Harper up the stairs to their room. She had fallen asleep again on the drive back to the house. He laid her on the bed and pulled up the covers before changing himself. Returning to the bed with a first aid kit, he looked at the cuts and welts on her wrists that she had mentioned. Reassuring himself that they were as minor as she had said, he cleaned them and applied an antiseptic ointment and covered them lightly with a gauze wrap. The stress of the evening plus the previous days hit him like a ton of bricks. Laken put the first-aid kit on the bedside stand before turning to join Harper in bed. In her sleep, she reached for him and let him gather her into his arms, surprising him. Tomorrow, they would deal with the aftermath of the kidnapping.

Harper slowly awoke to find herself wrapped in Laken's arms. She extricated an arm and brushed his cheek, then lips lightly with her fingertips. She felt him move and pulled back her hand, looking at his face to see him watching her.

"You don't have to stop, but how are your wrists?" he asked.

"Umm...they don't hurt. Thank you for taking care of them. Why aren't you at work?" Harper countered, scooting away from him. She had noticed the bandages on her wrists only after he had mentioned them, and she looked down.

Laken stretched and replied, "I've just worked five straight days, then I came back to find you gone. Why would I go to work today? I want to make sure you're okay. Plus, we have your doctor's appointment today, right?"

Harper had lost track of days. Today was the next prenatal appointment. It was right after lunch today rather than in the morning like before. "Yeah," she said, "It's at 1pm. What time is it now?"

Laken rolled over to look at the clock on the bedside stand. "It's almost 8:30."

"Oh, no!" exclaimed Harper. "The workers from the interior designer will be here soon. We need to get up."

Harper attempted to roll over, and Laken laughed to see her struggle to do so. "Stop laughing at me!" she commanded him. "You try getting up when there's a watermelon strapped to your middle."

Laken got out of bed, coming around and helping Harper up, still with a smile on his face. Harper turned away, obviously miffed at him as she made her way to the bathroom. He heard the shower turn on as he went to the dressing room to get himself dressed. Once ready, he headed downstairs to have the chef make breakfast. He would bring it up to Harper himself and eat with her after making sure the workers were all set.

Harper finished with her shower and changed into a clean set of clothes just in time to overhear Laken giving instructions to the workers for the nursery through the open bedroom door. She walked over to the door and glanced into the hallway.

"Harper, shouldn't you be lying down?" asked Laken.

She replied, "I was just checking to see if there was anything I needed to clarify for the nursery. Plus, I need to ask the chef about breakfast."

Laken explained, "I already ordered breakfast for us both, and it'll be ready in a couple of minutes. Sit down; I'll bring it up. You need to rest after yesterday's ordeal."

The reminder of the kidnapping caused her to stop and glance down at her wrists. Suddenly, everything that had happened overwhelmed her, and she cried. The sudden change in his wife startled Laken, but he stepped forward and wrapped her in his arms. He held her until she finished crying, rubbing her back to soothe her. Slowly, Harper's sobs quieted, and she lifted her head from his shoulder to wipe at her wet face.

"I'm fine now. You can let me go. I didn't mean to fall apart like that. I'm sorry." She said.

Laken scoffed. "Why are you apologizing? Someone kidnapped you. I'm surprised something like this didn't happen sooner. Now, I'm going to get breakfast. I'll be right back."

Harper headed to the sitting area to wait for Laken to bring the food. He joined her fairly quickly, and they both ate. While they ate, Laken watched over her to see if there were any more emotional effects from the kidnapping that showed. Once finished, Laken excused himself to take care of some things in the office while Harper laid back in bed. She found herself engrossed in an ebook that she had previously found unable to find of interest.

It was a fictional story about a woman who fell in love with a werewolf, but she didn't know that he was one. Harper found herself drawn into the story, finding similarities between the plot and her life. The book had many inaccurate details about werewolves, based on her research. She finished it that day and wondered if she should give grace to Laken the same that the heroine did in the ebook. The heroine had learned that her love was a werewolf and accepted him once he explained his side. She learned about his world and moved into the packhouse with him. Maybe Harper wasn't being accepting of Laken and needed to let him in more.

In the home office, Laken was in an emergency meeting with the werewolf council. He had texted the members when he had gone to get breakfast and set it up to be held virtually as he refused to leave the house or Harper. Laken informed the council of the kidnapping of Harper and Adria's involvement. Tatum, Raegan, and Colt followed up with their own accounts of being there as well. After hearing all the details, Paxton called for a vote on whether to allow human authorities to handle the matter. While it would seem this should be a werewolf matter, Harper's being a human plus the number of human laws that Adria had broken would mean that she would be in prison for life. It was enough to warrant its being out of the council's control. The council voted unanimously for the kidnapping to be handled by law enforcement. Laken logged off the virtual meeting and sighed. If only handling the kidnapping's aftermath were that simple.

That afternoon, Laken joined her again for lunch before they headed to the appointment. Soon they arrived at the appointment, which was routine, so it didn't take as long as the previous one. The doctor assured them that all was going well, even after the kidnapping. Harper's blood pressure continued to stay in the normal range with the rest she was taking. There were now only four more weeks until the baby's due date.

After dinner, Laken received a call saying that the police had apprehended Adria and her sidekick. They were being held at the local station. Laken had decided that letting the legal system deal with them both was the best way to keep Harper safe. Tatum had turned over all the evidence that he had collected, which was enough to put them both away for the kidnapping and attempted murder.

Over the next few days, Laken and Harper settled into a routine. Laken worked fewer hours to have breakfast and dinner with Harper each day. During the day, Harper would rest, read, and do research while he was at the office for those few hours.

Harper had made headway on her thesis and had enough to prove that werewolves existed. She had evidence that they survived until the late 1760s. There were enough manuscripts, records, art, and accounts from medieval times through the early 18th century to verify her hypothesis that were-wolves were real. In the early 18th century, though, they became extinct, but it was just conjecture. Harper had no solid confirmation of that yet. It was an unproven hypothesis and the next item on her list to find documentation for.

Lingering between them: The reason for Harper's departure was still unaddressed, a silence hanging heavy between them. The nursery was due to be completed in less than two weeks. The interior designer had been texting Harper photos of items that he had found for the nursery for approval. She had loved everything so far. Over dinner each evening, Harper updated Laken on the day's progress.

The day after Harper's 38-week appointment, the interior designer came in the morning for the last review and setup of the nursery. Laken took the afternoon off to come to the unveiling of the baby's room. He helped walk Harper down to the nurs-ery. With a flourish, the interior designer opened the door, leading them into the transformed room. Dominated by natural wood furniture and green painted walls, it had a natural feel to it. There was a nook with books and a rocking chair, as well as an area filled with stuffed animals.

"It's perfect," breathed Harper.

She and Laken walked around the nursery, explor-ing the place created for their child. They were both more than thrilled with the   interior designer and his team.

Harper turned to Laken and hugged him. "Thank you for doing this for our baby. It was your idea." She felt his love for their baby through his efforts at the nursery.

Chapter 14

A few days later, Harper realized that she and Laken had to have the talk that they'd been avoiding. They had less than two weeks until the baby was born. They could no longer dodge the conversation. Laken had already left to go to the office for the day, so she would bring it up after dinner that night.

After dinner in the sitting area, Harper wrung her hands in her lap and looked at them. Laken noticed and asked, "Is something wrong, moonflower?"

"We need to talk about why I left and everything," said Harper, looking up at him. "We've avoided talking about this and really need to do so before the baby is born."

Laken replied, "You're right. We do. Why don't you tell me what you want to say instead of my asking questions? I think that may be easiest."

Harper took a breath. She twisted her wedding ring on her finger as she spoke. "The day I found out I was pregnant was the day Adria showed up. Initially, I was upset about her, but you left, and I calmed down. Then I ran into her again. She tried to tell me again that she was your fiance and convince me to leave."

"That conniving bitch!" interjected Laken. Harper put a hand on his arm.

"Let me continue," she pleaded. He nodded, though he clenched his hands on his thighs.

"Adria also told me that..." Harper trailed off.

Laken asked, "What?"

"That you, she, and everyone here are werewolves," Harper continued, looking up at Laken and into his eyes.

His eyes widened at this revelation. This wasn't what he had expected to hear. *This was why she had left?*

Looking back down at her hands, Harper finished, "Adria also said that you would tire of me and later use me as a human sacrifice in a ceremony. I went through your office and found the drawer with a false bottom, hiding the ancient ritual book and other items. I was afraid of confronting you and finding out the truth. Knowing that I was pregnant, I couldn't take the chance that you would hurt the baby."

Laken slipped off the chair and onto the floor in front of Harper. He wrapped his hands around hers and kissed her knuckles. "Harper, I can't believe that this is why you left. I wish you had talked to me. I would have shared the whole truth with you."

Tearing her hands from his, Harper asked, "What is the truth, Laken?"

Laken took her face in his hands as he took a deep breath and said, "Yes, I'm a werewolf. But there is no way I'm going to tire of you. Nor do werewolf packs do any human sacrifice. I'll answer all questions for you that you have. Figuring out a way for me to tell you about me way before now was difficult. I never meant to hurt you. You're my mate. That means fate brought us together. It's why we have such a strong emotional and sexual attraction. That's also why I can guarantee I'll never tire of you."

Harper pulled back. "Why then would you have told me but never did? And what do you mean, mate?"

"We're not allowed to let humans know about us except in special circumstances like ours. Mates are like two people in love in the werewolf world. Except that it's a union that is fated by the Moon Goddess, and werewolves find each other through scent. In our case, only I could find you that way since you're a human. I realized you were my mate at the airport when I picked you up that day. But when we touch, I know you can feel the connection, too."

"But that doesn't answer why you never told me," reiterated Harper.

Laken clarified. "Once I heard you talk about your Master's thesis, I was afraid that you would have a bias because of the unfavorable outlook that exists about werewolves. I had hoped that after we got to know each other, then I could tell you and you would realize that werewolves were like humans in a lot of ways."

Reaching out to put a hand to his cheek, Harper said, "Oh, Laken, you're such a silly man for being smart. I can't believe you would think that I would believe propaganda. From my research, I've found out a lot about werewolves. It was fear for our baby that led me to leave because I didn't know if the human sacrifice was real or not. That wasn't something I had come across or seen disproved."

Laken leaned forward to hug his wife. "I would never hurt you or our child."

"I know that now. Before, we were still so new in our relationship that I didn't know that," replied Harper.

Smiling, Laken replied, "When you were kidnapped, my worry about losing either of you drove me crazy. How do you feel now about my being a werewolf?"

"Now, I have so many questions. Did Michael know you were a werewolf? Why do you live here in San Francisco? I read werewolf packs live in isolated areas away from humans." Harper shot off a slew of questions to her husband.

Laughing, Laken tried to answer her questions. "No, Michael didn't know. I couldn't break the rules and tell him the truth."

Laken reached out and ran his fingers down her face as he said this. Continuing, he answered her last question, "I started this pack when I was sixteen years old. When I was twelve, a war between our pack and another killed my parents. The other pack wiped out our pack. Rather than become a slave in the other pack, I became a rogue. I found a group of other rogues, and we became a sort of pack ourselves. Later, we settled here in San Francisco to finish school. I discovered many rogues were in the same situation as myself; they had become rogues out of desperation or losing their families. That is why I started a pack of rogues or for those who were being persecuted. Since I was the only Alpha among us, I became the leader of the new pack. It was hard at first because I didn't have money or property. We lived where we could and had to support ourselves. Later, I started Wolffang Enterprises and hired as many werewolves as I could, but also humans. I wouldn't turn down anyone who needed a job."

Harper had been listening intently throughout the entire explanation. Her eyes had gotten wider with each piece of information he revealed.

"We still don't follow the typical pack rules. We have no packhouse or grounds where all the werewolves live. I own the acreage outside of San Francisco where we found you. It's a place where anyone in the pack can go to change into their wolf form and go for a run in safety. The San Francisco Area werewolf pack is one of the largest packs in North America, both for the number of werewolves and physical area size that the pack covers. There are many who call it the Wolffang pack because of the connection between the pack and my business." finished Laken.

"This brings up more questions. Why didn't you tell me this before? And why did you let Adria stay at the house before? My werewolf research showed that people eradicated werewolves in the late 1760s.

Does this mean that instead of becoming extinct, they went underground?" Harper shot questions at him.

Laken laughingly replied, "I'll answer this final set of questions, then we'll save any remaining questions for tomorrow. I wanted you to be comfortable with me before telling you the truth. To become a true, full mate, there are three steps. We have yet to complete the final step. Plus, once you become my full mate, you'll become my Luna and share pack leadership with me. As you have discovered so far, explaining everything is quite a lot. Let's finish the complete discussion tomorrow. As for Adria, as the Alpha, I'm responsible for all the pack members. She requested a place to stay, and all know that I've guest rooms that are available if needed. She took advantage of that fact. I told her, she had two days to find a place to stay."

Taking a deep breath, Laken shared with Harper information that no human had ever heard. "And yes, werewolves went into hiding at the end of the 18th century. You're the only human to hear this. I'm giving you this knowledge, and you mustn't use it in your thesis."

Looking at Laken in surprise, Harper said, "Thank you for trusting me with this. I'll keep it safe."

"Now, enough talk. It's late. Let's go to bed," replied Laken. He helped her up from the chair and led her to the bed. He helped her change into her pajamas and settled under the covers before heading to the dressing room to change himself. Returning, he climbed into bed and snuggled up to his wife. He placed his hand over her very round stomach. Laken could feel the pup kicking and restless. He rubbed his hand around in soothing circles, trying to help settle his child down. Harper would have a hard time sleeping with all the movement going on.

Laken felt and heard a sigh from Harper as the pup slowly stopped moving. A few minutes later, Harper relaxed as she fell asleep. Soon, Laken did the same.

Chapter 15

THE next morning, Harper slept late and woke to find Laken still at home, which surprised her. He had waited to have breakfast with her, enjoying coffee in the office until she had awoken. The two of them still had a lot to discuss and clear up, so he had taken the day off. Laken brought in the breakfast tray and joined her on the bed to eat.

"Good morning, my moonflower," he said as he pecked her on the cheek.

Harper asked him, "Why are you still home? Usually you're at work by now."

Laken replied, "I told you last night that we would finish talking today, so I took the day off. I didn't feel that it would be fair for you to wait until later to finish having questions answered. First, let's eat. You and the pup need food."

"Pup?" Harper questioned.

Laken grinned at her. "Yes, that's what we were-wolves call our young. It'll be interchangeable with baby and child since our little one will be half human."

The two ate for a while before Laken said, "Harper, we haven't talked about names. Do you have any you like and have thought of?"

Harper told him, "I've a few that I like." She opened the bedside-stand drawer and pulled out a notepad. Handing it to Laken, he read the list on it out loud.

"Gunnar, Cade, Jamis, Beckett, Briggs, Bryson, Hudson."

He said each of the names out loud again with his last name, wanting to hear how they sounded. Once he did this, he told Harper, "I like Briggs or Cade the best. What do you think?"

She smiled at him. "Briggs was one of my favorites, so I think that's the one."

Reaching over to lay his hand on her belly, Laken leaned close and spoke to their son, "What do you think, little one? Do you like it? Briggs Howlkind?"

Almost as if he was answering in the affirmative, there was a kick in Laken's hand. Laughing, Harper told her husband, "I think he agrees."

"Moonflower, are you done eating?" asked Laken.

Harper replied, "For now. I feel like my stomach is being smashed by our son, and I can't eat as much right now. Leave me the fruit, and I'll snack on it later."

After cleaning up the breakfast, Laken set the tray outside the suite door. Returning to the bed, he pulled Harper to his side, so she was leaning against him. "I promised to finish our talk last night, so let's do that. I need to tell you the last piece of the mate bond and about the responsibilities of a Luna. You may know some of this from your research, but I want to go over it. Within the pack, a Luna acts as a mother figure. She's the head of the she-wolves and helps nurture the pack. The Luna also sits on the werewolf council with the Alpha. She helps the Alpha decide and rule the pack."

Harper listened to this and tried to wrap her head around what she would need to do. She had read about some of the Luna responsibilities when she had researched the pack member roles; however, hearing them and knowing it would be her respon-sibility were two different things. *Could she do this? Would the pack accept her?* She wondered.

"Three things complete the mate bond: scenting, sex, and marking. We have done two of the three," explained Laken.

Harper looked at him questioningly. "Marking?"

"Werewolves bite each other, injecting pheromones that mark them as claimed. My wolf and I've wanted to mark you since day one. It has taken so much effort not to do so. Both before you left and after you came back." Laken admitted this to Harper.

Gulping, Harper repeated, "Bite?"

Continuing, Laken said, "For werewolves, it doesn't hurt. In fact, I've heard it can be more of an aphrodisiac. I don't know what it's like for humans. But if we do it during sex, I'm sure it wouldn't hurt much."

"How would I mark you, though?" asked Harper. "You said werewolves mark each other."

"You can bite me anytime you want," said Laken with a smirk. "If you want to do it every day to let others know I'm yours, I'll let you."

Harper looked at him in disbelief, but her heart was actually beating erratically in her chest. The thought of biting him every day sounded both delightful and wicked.

"Last night you said that mates are like people in love. And you keep calling me moonflower, but you've never said you love me. Yet here you are, talking about marking me. What do I mean to you — just a physical attraction?" demanded Harper.

Laken looked at her in disbelief. Here he was explaining the mating bond and wanting to mark her, yet he was messing it all up. "No! For werewolves, we wait forever for our mate. It's who the Moon Goddess has fated us to be, the person we're to spend our life with. When you disappeared, I ceased to live. My other half was gone. I was so scared that I would never find you again and would be a shell of a person forever. I love you so much that I was afraid that if I told you, I would scare you away. That's why I call you my moonflower. Because you're the flower that the Moon Goddess gave to me, a gift to cherish." He confessed.

Reaching for his face, Harper put a palm on his cheek. "I was afraid that you had only married me because Michael had asked you to. While we were lovers, it was all for the sake of responsibility. To find out that you love me is almost unreal, because I love you, too."

"If you marked me now, would it hurt the baby?" she asked hesitantly, looking down at her hands.

Laken smiled at her tenderly, tilting her chin so he could look her in the eyes. "No, my love, it won't hurt our son."

Harper pulled her hair back from her neck and tilted her head to the side. "I'm ready then."

Laken pulled Harper's face to his, then kissed her deeply. Once she was gasping, he bent her head to the side, opened his mouth and bit down where her neck met her shoulder. She moaned as he broke the skin. The completion of the mate bond made Enzo ecstatic with the marking done. The mark on Harper's neck gave him a feeling of ownership and happiness to know that if anything happened to her now, he would know about it.

Harper's head fell back when Laken sat up again. The marking caused her eyes to glaze over slightly. The feeling that had come with it was unexpected. She reached for him and looked at him with a question on her face.

"Just do what feels natural," Laken advised.

Harper reached for Laken as he bent over her with his own neck exposed to her. She laid her mouth on his skin, opened it, and bit down. Feeling the skin break, she moaned, licked the blood off, then heard him moan. Sitting back, she looked at the mark now on Laken's neck. She felt a sort of pleasure in seeing it, knowing that it meant he was hers.

Glancing at Laken, she saw him looking at her with hooded eyes. She leaned forward, her own eyelids lowering into a smoldering look as she kissed him on the neck, near where she had marked him. Hearing a hiss from him, she pulled at his shirt, which he took off willingly. Harper ran her hands over his chest, then around his neck to pull him down to her. Taking the lead, she plunged her tongue into his mouth, sucking at his and then nipping at his lower lip.

Laken groaned, pulling away to pull off her nightgown. He palmed her breasts, still amazed and thrilled at their larger size. Remembering how she had told him they were more sensitive now, he took a nipple gently into his mouth, rolling it between his teeth but not biting down, then laving it.

Harper moaned in delight, making Laken smile. He switched his attention to the other breast while his hand slid between them to the apex of her thighs. Feeling how wet and ready she was, Laken rolled over and shucked off his pants. He knew her climax would come quickly and fast, and so would his with the marking they had just completed.

Turning back to his wife, Laken took a pillow and placed it under her hips. He had read that this was an excellent position for women in their last months of pregnancy. Leaning over, he passionately kissed Harper while he aligned himself with her opening.

Harper gasped at the change of depth and penetration as Laken filled her. Also, it felt more intense than previously, which must be in her mind, right? Laken began to move, in then out, and she moved with him. Her muscles tightened, and she could feel herself breaking already. She grasped Laken's forearms as waves of ecstasy washed over her.

Laken felt Harper quaking around him, and he raced to the finish just behind her, pumping his hips a few more times. He held himself over her not to press on her belly, with his head resting on her chest while he caught his breath. Once he recovered enough to move again, he withdrew and moved to her side.

Harper took his hand in hers when he placed it on her stomach. "Why did that feel so...different?" She asked.

"Sex between two marked mates is beyond the physical. It's a connection between both our bodies and souls." explained Laken. He kissed her forehead and pulled her close to him.

Harper rolled over a bit and then snuggled next to him. Her mate. That would take a bit to get used to. For now, the revelations, the marking, and the mating had worn her out. Laken encouraged her to nap while he got up to take care of some things.

When Harper woke up, Laken shared with her his decision to turn over most of the daily running of Wolffang Enterprises to Tatum. It would be a slow transition that would take place over the next several months. Shocked yet delighted by this, Harper could only ask him if he was sure of this decision.

"Are you sure this is what you want to do?" asked Harper.

Laken assured her. "Yes, I am. I've been running the business non-stop for ten years. Almost losing you made me realize how important you and our child are to me. I don't want to miss any more moments with either of you. I'll still be part of the board and   the majority shareholder. But I don't need to be involved in the daily running of Wolffang Enterprises. My preoccupation with your disappearance led Tatum to manage the company during that time. He can competently take it over."

Leaning over, he placed his head on the swell of her stomach and turned to place a kiss on it. "I'll always be here for you and Briggs, as well as any other pups we may have. Losing my parents as a teenager, I know that family is the most significant people in my life. I know you feel the same too."

Harper kissed the top of his head. "I wonder if Michael knew you were my mate. He's in heaven, smiling at us in love with a baby almost here."

Epilogue

THE day of the Luna ceremony and presentation of their son began full of sunshine. The werewolf council had scheduled the dual rituals for sundown at the Golden Gate Park Bandshell for the night of a full moon after the baby was a month old. Full moons were significant times for werewolf ceremonies.

Briggs Michael Howlkind had been born two days after his due date. It had been a long but healthy birth. Laken had been there for Harper throughout the entire ordeal. He was proud of his wife and absolutely enamoured of his newborn son. The staff at his house had smiled and laughed as they watched him carry Briggs around on his first day home, showing the boy around the house.

Now their son was five and a half weeks old, and they couldn't imagine life without him. He had his father's brown hair but Harper's blue eyes. They had been told to expect them to change as all newborns had blue eyes, but so far they hadn't done so. He had taken to nursing like a champ and regained his birth weight in less than a week. Harper had also slimmed back down quickly, shedding the baby weight.

For the ceremony, Laken had ordered a silk caftan gown for her to wear. Briggs had his own infant-size suit that matched his father's. The family would look like the werewolf royalty that they were.

After sundown, they headed to the Bandshell park with Tatum and his mate, Elsie. Briggs had fallen asleep on the drive. Harper and Laken hoped he stayed that way for most of the ceremony time. They had worked hard to get him into a sleep routine. The timing of the ceremony could ruin what they had just put into place.

Nearby in other parts of the park, the Outside Lands Music Festival was taking place, but werewolves who were part of the local police force had set up a barricade to prevent partygoers from coming near the ceremony. The festival would mask the sounds from inside the bandshell spreading.

The night itself was perfect for the outdoor ceremony. The sky was clear with no chance of rain, so there was a perfect view of the full moon. It was one of the warmer days of the month of August, with the temperature hovering in the mid-60s for the evening. Every San Francisco Area werewolf pack member who could was planning to attend, along with Alphas and Lunas from nearby packs as well. This was the Lycan event of the year, and the weather had cooperated with the occasion.

The Elders, Wells, and Jora, began with the Luna ceremony first. They had Harper stand in front of the pack and recite the vows, where she pledged to take care of the pack members and be true to the Alpha. The Elders typically included a werewolf marriage ceremony, but they omitted it because Laken and Harper had already been legally married under human law for almost a year.

The pack members clapped and came to present Harper with gifts that had been prepared for her. She graciously accepted these, which she would look through later at home. The visiting Alphas and Lunas next shook Harper's hand and wished her their best. Some also presented gifts.

Soon, Wells showed it was time to move on to the Briggs' pack introduction. He had been watching and measuring the moon. The timing of this presentation was important so that it was done when the moon was twenty degrees above the horizon. The werewolf ancient text declared that when a future Alpha was given to the Moon Goddess at that precise lunar measurement, "This is a child marked for destiny, who stands at the edge of emotional initiation. Watched by ancestors and shadowed by fate, he must grow into leadership guided by intuition and moonlight." It was an honored and sacred moment in werewolf culture.

Laken lifted Briggs from his car seat, careful not to wake the infant. He lifted his son over his head as Wells sang a chant invoking the Moon Goddess to watch over the future Alpha and keep him safe from harm.

"Moon Mother, Silver Light Watch our Alpha through the night.

Child of fate, born of the moon, Guard his soul, protect his name.

By the stars and
shadowed   pine,
Mark his path with
signs divine.

Shield his heart,
his strength, his
soul, Until he rises,
fierce and whole.

Lend your glow
to guide his way,
Keep all evil wolf at
bay.

By your grace and
ancient art, Let no
blade nor curse
impart.

Luna bright, with
wisdom deep, Cra-

dle him in dream-
less sleep.

Until the time the
crown is worn —
Keep him safe till
he is sworn.

So we howl, so we
vow, Moon above,
hear us now."

At the end of the chant, the entire pack then fell to its knees and howled for the pup in recognition of his future role. Tears fell down Laken's face at the acceptance of his son by the pack. Bringing the infant down from above his head, he cradled the baby against his chest and kissed him on his forehead.

Laken whispered a blessing he remembered hearing his father say to him: "By blood and moon, I bless you, my son. May your heart be fierce, your spirit unbroken. Walk with honor, lead with strength. The pack stands behind you—always. You are my legacy. You are our future."

Harper encircled Laken's waist with her arm as Laken finished speaking the blessing to their son. She kissed Briggs' head, then Laken. She, the Luna and Bride of Wolffang.

About the Author

JS Williams writes contemporary, historical, and paranormal romance, blending emotional depth with unforgettable characters. Her debut novel, *Bride of Wolffang*, was published in July 2025.

A lifelong Michigander, JS grew up on the Sunrise Side and now lives in Grand Rapids, Michigan, with her husband and their two teenage sons. When she's not writing, she works as a school occupational therapist, supporting students in special education—a career she has devoted more than twenty-five years to.

JS is passionate about making reading accessible. She incorporates dyslexia-friendly fonts, thoughtful spacing, and visual elements into her books to support readers of all abilities.

When she isn't immersed in storytelling, you'll find her reading, traveling, working on projects for her

LLC, or spending time with family and friends. A tattooed, introverted Gen Xer with a love for 80s music, JS brings both heart and authenticity to every story she tells.

www.ingramcontent.com/pod-product-compliance
Lightning Source LLC
Chambersburg PA
CBHW021201310726
48971CB00002B/727